DILETTANTES
AND
HEARTLESS MANIPULATORS

DILETTANTES
AND
HEARTLESS MANIPULATORS

NATE WAGGONER

Snow Goose Press
www.snowgoosepress.com

Parts of this book were published in Sparkle & Blink, TheFanzine.com,
Makeout Creek, MilkMade, and in a split zine from The Gorilla Press.

ISBN: 978-0-9964262-0-6 (paperback)

First edition published by Snow Goose Press, 2015.
Printed in the United States of America by CreateSpace.

Cover art and jacket design © 2015 by Nate Waggoner

Snow Goose Press
El Cerrito, CA; Brooklyn, NY
www.snowgoosepress.com

This book is for Hope
and for Amanda
and for Dante.

"…How can an animal faith in one's blear guiding star be regarded as something peculiar and rare?"

-Vladimir Nabokov, "Tyrants Destroyed."

Dilettantes
and
Heartless Manipulators

TABLE OF CONTENTS

Chapter 1: The Right Profile

Jimmy Sincere
26
Bluffberg, VA
January, 2012

What I'm Doing with My Life:

I am an aspiring rapper but most nights instead of making beats I drink a 40 and watch Ultimate Fighting at my mother's house where I live and I regret at age ten calling her a hellbeast because she is at least as tolerant as my ex-wife, who is now in France, where there are Frenchmen, and who used to break car windows with me, who cheered me on during the Extreme Waffle Challenge, who on 9/11/01 in Spanish class when the tragedy was announced hollered out, "No me *gus*-taaa" in like a sing-song and no one laughed but me. Whose cat, Famous Murderer, I saved from drowning. Who I drove away by calling people Nazis at her office Christmas party and by touching her breasts in front of her parents, the former of which she still believes (I know because I sometimes call Chloe in France on my mother's phone and she still picks up pretty frequently, I suspect because she knows how guilty I'll feel about it later when Mom is going over the phone bill and says nothing but sighs; that's how they both operate.) contributed to her being downsized, and which latter was apparently the last straw with her parents who had been threatening for three years to cut her off if she and I planned on remaining married (they paid for the divorce; I honestly didn't know they didn't like me). I'm saying I *drove her into poverty*, ladies, and she had to take this PeaceCorps thing helping the little stripe-shirted mimelings of the, I guess, bad parts on the outskirts of Paris.

I proposed to her junior year of college. It was the day after the day that it occurred to me that girls only hook up anonymously with dudes of a certain height. I'd love to have tons of anonymous sex, but I've never had any anonymous sex because if you're my height or shorter, or maybe even like a few inches taller than me, girls have to be in love with you before they sleep with you. Somewhere in Nevada there's an ancient statue of unknown origin, like Easter Island except it looks more like a Bob's Big Boy-type character I think, a potbellied, smiling lad extends his arm at about 6'2", and underneath the arm it says in every human language that has ever existed or ever will exist, "You Must Be This Tall to Be A Sexually Promiscuous Man."

I wish I had known about that statue before I got these three tattoos.

Not to say I didn't love her, I did. But I also love strawberry-rhubarb pie and Mortal Kombat and the rock band Journey and my possibly schizophrenic friend, Matthew Elmer, who at one point tried to burn down the apartment we had together after an argument over preferred cereal brands. Maybe what was really important was that I needed her to make informed decisions about my life and to show me how to do basic things. Let me put it this way: if there are any parents reading this, and you're thinking about raising your kids as like a reaction to the hard times you yourself have had, like because you had to learn to fend for yourself and you didn't like it, and you want your kids to never have to worry about anything? Please don't do it that way. That's how my mom did it, and it's absolutely not worth it for kids like me, just because of the number of times your kid will end up embarrassing himself at like a 7-Eleven having a credit card and actually not knowing how it works, for instance, like handing the card to the man behind the counter and watching him point to the credit card machine your kid is supposed to swipe his card through, and your kid is like, "No, you don't understand, I want to pay for something with my credit card, I'm not interested in whatever that little screen with the shallow vertical little trench on the side there is," and the man behind the counter will be like, "Swipe it through, please," and your kid will be like, "No, you doofus, I'm trying to pay for this bag of Extreme Sour Gummies and these cigars with a credit card, so please take the card and do whatever it is you do with the card to make the money thing happen."

Or the time when your little darling will have to ask his or her college roommate not only how to boil water on the stove, but how to tell when the water is boiling.

And don't even get me started on food poisoning. You can't convince me that a destitute child in Uganda, or somewhere, would envy the amount of food poisoning I used to accidentally induce on myself and on my guests before Chloe and I lived together. Parents basically have to make a choice on the day their kid is born: do they want to teach their kid about money and food and clothes, or do they want their kid to end up in the hospital getting his stomach pumped at twenty-three (with no health insurance, obviously) because he tried to make a bagel.

So that's why I wanted to marry her—that, and because of that sex statue leering at me in the desert night. You're not so tough.

I Couldn't Live Without:

Now I eat all my mother's food. I live with her and my younger brother Elvis, who never left, and who writes fan fiction all day. I'm twenty-six and broke, and also I am forbidden to eat any of Elvis's mac and cheese or tuna. And my mother doesn't consume anything except Brie off a butter knife and pinot grigio. She is callused and gaunt and lives on disability. Dad died falling down the stairs when I was too young to remember. Anyway, so I mostly eat whatever's available. Elvis never eats leftovers, and he leaves his mac and cheese uncovered in the fridge, and it turns red and tastes sour. I will find the one thing left in the produce drawer, a red onion, say, and pare off the fuzzy parts and eat it raw. I eat spoonfuls of mayo until I feel adequately sick. The mayo sometimes sticks to my scruffy facial hair and I enjoy it all day, potential romantic partner who is reading this. Once I found an old box of Price Club microwave popcorn and none of the bags could pop quite right anymore—about half of the kernels popped and the bags would get burned on the side, and I would open the bags and, making a puppet face with my hand, grab as many popped or unpopped kernels as possible and stuff them into my mouth, burning both hand and mouth in the process.

It's exhausting to live like this, to be me. I need ten hours of sleep a night so I can get up and fume and starve and masturbate three times a day and get into fights with people on the Internet or in the parking lot of Trader Joe's. It takes all my strength.

At this point, I think my mother is trying to starve me out. She has the advantage of never being hungry, but I have the advantage of the willingness to eat her food, thus resulting in a greater potential of starvation for her. When she does eat, she sucks the food up, inhales it, like an Italian mobster, her only delight is in the destruction of the food, not in the taste or the texture or in the feeling of filling herself.

We were always the kind of family who not only had some emergency happening all the time, but if you came anywhere near us, we would be forced to coerce or guilt or cajole or browbeat you into helping out in some capacity: a cat was sick, Elvis injured himself trying to jump his bike off a ramp he made, I got us kicked out of a restaurant by standing up and shouting Biggie lyrics. Right now we're at an all-time low of three cats, the high being twelve. Cats that would constantly shit and knock things over and eat human food and other objects left around, to the point where we even designated a bathroom and another room just to be, basically, The Rooms Where Litterboxes Are, the cat's bathrooms, which I think, I hope, no other family has ever done. Cats get old and their aim gets terrible and they get the feces and litter stuck in their paws and they track it all through the house.

We keep chickens in a city where urban farming is pretty much unheard of and where everyone seems to work for a website called Zazz even though no one can really articulate what it does. Mom gets up at six every morning and feeds and yells at the chickens, calls them li'l sluts. She goes to bed at 9 p.m., a glass of white wine having taken its nightly toll on her system in every usual way, except for building up a tolerance to the effects of a single glass of wine. That wine held a special fascination for Elvis and I as kids, colored and seemingly textured the same as our life-giving appy juice, but causing Mom to fall asleep and giggle and yell. Mom put herself through college waiting tables— on rollerskates, she'd always remind us—until she could get a job as an eighth grade English teacher, which, apparently, you could do back in those days with just a B.A. in English and no teaching experience and a foul mouth and cat hair all over your shirt. She talks about Proust, and through her Southern accent, affects sort of an English accent on the pronunciation of certain words like "disgust," although I guess that's a word that lends itself to that.

Back to the food: there *used* to be food. Remember I said we never had to cook or learn anything or do anything? It's true. She did it all herself, and there was angel hair pasta with the little canned clam chunks, and peanut butter and marshmallow Fluff, and tuna melts, and Cream of Wheat with the raspberry drizzle dripped on top in the shape of a heart on Valentine's Day. I moved in here after Chloe left, and the one time I managed to go to a '90s party and make out with a girl, named Tara, and bring her back to my mother's place and sneak her into my room, Mom stormed in halfway through and kicked Tara out, made her walk home, and told me, "Ah never wanted you." So I guess what I'm saying with this profile is, uh, good luck.

I Spend a Lot of Time Thinking About:

When my friend Daniel Fairchild and I were twelve, we would walk around town, trying to find a woman who would let us both have sex with her at the same time. We had seen this website, tagteam.biz, in which two men, Bearman and The Disgusto, approached women on the street, beguiled them, and always did it so that Bearman would receive fellatio and The Disgusto would penetrate the woman from behind. They would tell jokes during the sex acts. We thought these guys were cool. I think we both saw ourselves as Disgustos, though. Every week Daniel's dad would pick me up and drop us off at the Downward Oaks Shopping Center, playing The Beatles on the car stereo, sometimes offering quiet but slightly snide criticism to individual Beatles if he felt like skipping a song, for example, "Eh, not your best one, George." We'd walk around and if we saw somebody we knew from school, we'd even tell them our plan. "Cool, can I join?" asked potential schizophrenic Matthew Elmer, but he still cried a lot. He was worse than us. We told him to take a hike and we felt cool.

We weren't interested in girls our own age, only milves and high school girls. College girls were pretty sparse around old Downward Oaks, and we were pretty sure we couldn't have convinced Mr. Fairchild to drop us off at Bluffberg Tech for the night. The teenagers—like sixteen-year-olds?—wore jeans and little gray rock band t-shirts that actually fit them, and they had slightly better skin than we did, no braces, and smoked *cigarettes*—cigarettes smelled like my grandmother's house to me still because they were *killing* her, but your brain doesn't take into account that kind of ambiguity when sorting between good and bad smells. To me, it was just a good smell. In the hands of older girls, they were both comforting and stunningly romantic. Sixteen-year-old girls, to us, seemed like the great minds of our time, luminaries, visiting dignitaries from the planet Sophistication. We sat there, daring each other for hours to talk to these girls. Eventually Daniel got a girlfriend. I wanted to ask him to ask her if we could Eiffel Tower her, but her name was Chelsea and she was on the Model UN, so.

I think about it pretty often, though, especially when I, like, use tagteam.biz. The women rarely make repeat appearances but are typically of the same porny type as they were when I was a kid, and the jokes are the same, but both Bearman and The Disgusto seem markedly more weary and haggard and obviously drunk and unvirile.

What I'm Really Good At:

Chapter 2: Portrait of the Artist as a Manchild

Jimmy thinks: it is so fucking corny they built this campfire. Like, they *lit*erally all came out here, Josie's friends from Apartheid, the clothing store she used to work at, they all came out in their moms' Corollas and congregated out in the actual *woods* as, like, a thing to do, and the worst part is he is here with them. He has not only agreed to do this, to be here this whole night with this dumb campfire, but to actually come and is therefore himself now one of them, the cutesy fire-appreciators. They drove out here with super-flammable DuraLogs and poured stuff on it and shoved newspapers in there—they *brought old newspapers* out here, girls in little white blouses and big dangly necklaces and dudes in Mickey Mouse sweatshirts and scraggly beards. Working and freezing and building while saying things like, "Oh word?" and "Yeah, he's in grad school now." Twenty-six years old and here he is.

Somebody brought and is passing around a 24-pack of Miller High Lives and Jimmy has drunk six of them. Jimmy is wearing a big white fake fur coat with a white t-shirt under it and black jeans. He has a gold chain around his neck. He is mean-muggin' like his name was Walter White, his jaw protruding like an inch. Josie is his boy Phil's girlfriend. Jimmy is a short guy but Josie is very small and has wiry arms and a big butt and long curly fake-red hair. She is wearing a mustard-yellow dress and purple tights and a jean jacket. She nudges his knee with hers and says, "How you feelin', Jimmy?"

"I was told Phil would be here," he says, and immediately feels bad. But also, it was kind of funny, right? She seems unaffected by it. She's used to that kind of treatment from him.

Some guy next to Jimmy, in a contemptible kitty-cat t-shirt—like what are you trying to prove?—starts trying to appeal to Jimmy's interests.

"So you're a rapper?" the dude says.

"Trying to be, yeah."

"What are like your influences?"

"Hey, does anybody have any bug spray?" Jimmy raises his voice, addressing the group in general. They laugh, because it's February. He doesn't know why he said that either. It is a special kind of humid cold out, like you're swimming in cold water.

Now they're, swear to God, talking about their phones and the different shit their phones can do.

"This one? You can sing into it? And it tells you the name of the song."

"Oh yeah?" Jimmy says. "Does your phone know this song?"

He starts crooning plaintively, and everyone looks at him patiently, condescendingly, like they have full faith some great punch line is coming, one they will all get and laugh appreciatively at, and Jimmy wants this too, but then he launches into a melodic tirade about what a bunch of boring bastards they all are, instead. The girl with the app actually keeps holding her phone out and recording. Jimmy starts to storm off, kicks some leaves, moves slightly back towards the fire to kick the log he'd been sitting on, then starts back into the woods again. Josie pauses, takes another drink from her Miller High Life, stands up, dusts her dress, nods curtly at her friends, and runs after Jimmy. Jimmy stops at the crest of a hill and Josie catches up with him.

"I don't see why you have to act like that just because Phil's not here," she stammers. Jimmy puts his hand on Josie's chin and moves his face towards her, lips bulging like a goof. She smacks his hand away, looking more annoyed than shocked.

"Why not?" Jimmy demands. The "t" in "not" comes out forcefully, a petulant near-fricative.

"God, you are such a pain-in-th'-*dick* sometimes, Jimmy." She starts walking off towards the stupid campfire. Jimmy keeps standing there.

"Why not, though!" She's out of sight now. "Hey, I thought you guys *liked* me!"

•

Josie, in her room at her desk covered in little plastic figurines and ornaments she's found, wonders what it would have been like if she had done the unthinkable and allowed Jimmy to kiss her. Would the tender side she knows he has, because she watched *Toy Story 3* with him, have come out, and would he have softly kissed her neck and run his hands up and down her skinny midsection? Or would he have just put her up against a tree like a cop arresting a suspect and gotten her face all prickly and pulled her underwear down? She finds her thoughts wandering pleasantly—aw, shit—to the latter. Doin' it with Jimmy. She'd like him to bite her ear, and she'd slap his face. They could bone on public transit. He could splay her legs on his mom's kitchen counter, and she could grab a chair and hit him over the head with it like a wrestler, his eyes glazed and his torso thrusting weakly but not missing a beat. She could set the bed on fire and hold him down, bobbing fervently on top of him until she climaxed at the exact moment they both became enveloped in flames that would leave them hideously mutilated for the rest of their lives, mutant freaks, wandering around scaring people and stealing their cars. She becomes short of breath thinking about it. She starts to feel faint, like when you take an Excedrin without eating. Her heart is trying to punch its way out.

Phil walks in the room and hands her a cucumber-slices-and-cream-cheese sandwich, cut in triangles with the crust removed from the rosemary bread. Phil buys rosemary and regular, for Chrissakes, because he knows she likes it, and she always ends up eating his food when she's over at his place, and what do you do about *that?*

.

Jimmy is parallel parking on an incline by his friend Trevor's house. He promises himself he will get there and talk to everyone like they're human beings, and play Apples to Apples according to the rules, and even suggest the game if they are not playing it, because he is funny when he plays it, and the limitations of the game and the phrases on the cards force him into a crowd-pleasing vein of safe humor, jokes that are appropriate for the situation. Jimmy hopes to see: skinny girls in wraparound bras and big see-through shirts like nets, too much raccoonish or Native American-y eye makeup, or no makeup at all, stringy hair, a girl who brings her dog everywhere. They might go to another party after, some paranoid douchebag's place where

Jimmy and another person could do coke in a soapless bathroom where the lock doesn't quite work and people are mad he's taking so long. All around him, everyone seems to be having sex constantly (maybe not Josie and Phil). When Jimmy was married he felt like every associate he had, every coworker, everyone he'd gone to school with, good-looking or not, seemed to be regularly engaged in anonymous, hilariously meaningless encounters, threesomes, foursomes, semi-public-type situations, Internet stuff, hookups inside bookstores, affairs, arrangements, triangles, experiments, entanglements, only intimated and intuited, some smugly chill and some smugly dramatic, and Jimmy, despite his general satisfaction with life with Chloe, was compelled to try and ask for as many details as possible, trying to seem subtle but only coming off as hungry and creepy, envious of other people's glamorous-seeming problems but only dimly aware of the specifics.

The dusk sky seems small and constricting: his ambition is a size perfectly appropriate for such a limited purple and pink and gray sky. How could elementary school, or, in her better moods, Mom, have told him to dream big when all that truly looms is this perfect inverted bauble of consolidated nothingness, lusts to sate, consciousness to eliminate, now forming tendrils of fog and reaching down at him? His mom's car's heater rattles.

He gets there and everyone is fixated on the old *Swamp Thing* cartoon on Trevor's TV, and this guy Willy, who Jimmy doesn't really know and who has blond hair and messy facial hair and a hoodie, is passing a bong around. Jimmy knows this will make him weird, that he can't handle it the way everyone else can, especially not from this powerful bong with little glass wings on the side, but he takes a hit anyway. All hope of venturing out is destroyed; everyone's adherence to Earth's gravity is now wildly out of proportion to his or her actual mass. Only Jimmy finds himself in the kitchen, skulking around like some primitive creature. Often he feels like there is the real Jimmy, who is struggling to control this monstrous puppet of himself, but it's the puppet that's making jokes about his penis (their penis?) and that tried to kiss Josie last week and that opens the freezer now and takes out a thing of Pizza Bites that doesn't belong to him. This rubbery flesh, these goofball fuck you clothes, the slight lisp, this nose (which even his mother makes jokes about, and it's her nose): all necessary to present to people in order to get what he wants, even though he doesn't deserve what he wants, which is apparently Pizza Bites. Applying for jobs, asking his mom for money, once even asking his then-in-laws for money, spitting game at girls and just *sweating* and *breathing*... Hope Jimmy is still down there, underneath the puppet, and will one day escape and be free to be beautiful and well-mannered and loved.

.

The guy lying still on his back as the light comes in gray like old coffee has a cool beard and is impressively tall and is not circumcised(!), Josie remembers. He had kept his big black t-shirt on the whole time. She looks at her legs and how pale they are. She is wearing decidedly unseductive pink-and-white striped panties. The guy, Noah, is still asleep. She puts her jeans on and leaves the room without saying anything, as she assumes people do in these situations.

Your twenties are a moral cocoon.

The main room has a probably unintentional coral scheme and a roommate is watching a teen melodrama. The couch, and thus his back, are luckily turned towards her. He doesn't look up until she opens the front door, and she catches a brief glimpse of his dirty brown hair and the slope of his forehead. She is pretty sure it is not anyone she recognizes. This, people are fond of saying around here, is a small town.

It had not been the cataclysmic sex she had been fantasizing about having with Jimmy. She and Noah had needed to walk way too far in the cold to get to his house, and halfway there he'd started discoursing on his admiration for the poetry of Ralph Waldo Emerson and she decided she fucking hated him. There was some lazy making out and unearned hard fucking (on his part) and she was trying not to fall asleep by the time he came. This encounter has been a precautionary measure, an adult decision to do something terrible so she wouldn't have to want to anymore.

Don't tell anyone, but Josie listens to those inspirational tapes. The one she's listening to now is called, "How to Get What You Want Out of Life Without Making the Same Mistakes Your Parents Did." She is not sure if she is following its advice correctly or not.

.

Phil is picking up his rosemary bread and his whole wheat and a young guy in a suit in front of him in line is taking his time shamelessly hitting on the super-beautiful Hispanic girl behind the counter, and she is giggling and blushing. Everyone is so selfish, Phil thinks, even me. I'm selfish for even thinking it, for not recognizing the rights of others to be selfish. The cashier can help the next in line. Not that it matters, but this girl is really radiant, and Phil knows he will make an absolute goober of himself right now just talking to her, despite his devotion to Josie. He thinks, Just try not to make any disgusting noises with your mouth. She asks if he wants paper or plastic and he takes too long to respond because he's not thinking about it, he's thinking about how he hasn't responded yet. He mumbles, "Plastic," and she doesn't hear him, so he repeats himself too loud, as if he was mad, but he's not mad.

He goes home and punishes himself for the awkwardness of the encounter by listening to a CD of Halloween songs where little kids shriek along enthusiastically in the choruses. His dad calls and says, "Your mother and I are thinking about going to Outback *Snake*house, heh-heh." Phil politely declines. Josie comes over and they watch this biopic about young Emerson for some reason. She holds him and makes him feel smooth and bright.

·

One night the following week, Josie is back in the unintentional coral living room/ kitchen area. Noah, three other tall bearded men in jeans and flannel, and one quiet girl who looks like a mousier Jane Birkin, no competish really (Josie catches herself thinking this way and decides she's fine with it), are there too. Noah keeps putting his arm around Josie. A Ouija board lies abandoned on the floor amid cups of cheap Merlot and brightly-colored plastic plates off of which they had eaten (fantastic) tempeh and greens. Josie holds court. "Starting with Part 2, all of Jason's victims were in love with him. Think about it." Her company appears perplexed, compelled. "They drive out to visit him. They dress up like him and spook each other, sometimes just before fucking! Like some courtship ritual! They're fans just like we are. And *then*, it's even more blatant in the 3-D one, because you have axes and harpoons and shit literally *flying* at you from their point of view." Josie leans forward in the big wooden chair she sits in, poking the air with her index finger. She wants to talk forever. She wants to talk like her mom gets to talk at town council meetings.

Noah thinks: I mustn't beam with excess magnanimity, lest Josie see. How she talks at length and with éclat about cinema! And yet, how she has also revealed her inner, vulnerable self to me. She has told of falling off a tractor in her very early childhood ("Remember getting hurt when you were a kid? Everything was so much worse because it was unprecedented...") and of her parents' recent separation, of old boyfriends, all with similar brash grace.

Noah has known, and suffered infatuation with, five girls of whom she now reminds him. They all had red hair, all could dance in a way his gawky frame could not keep up with, all had been very much spoken for when Noah knew them: married, engaged, pre-engaged, living with someone, wearing a promise ring... Just once he'd like to be considered deserving of the whole attention of such an effervescent presence.

The doorbell rings. Josie turns to see a long-haired roommate open the door and greet Phil warmly. Phil has never introduced Josie to any of these people. Had Phil had some class with this dude? What was his name? Jeff? Ice spreads along the ocean floor of her gut; butterflies prepare for hibernation.

Phil sees Josie and cocks his head to the left theatrically in friendly confusion the way a dog does. He smiles and waves cutely. She rises and walks towards him, and he suddenly does something he's never done as long as she's known him—he takes her and gives her a great shameless rough smooch, more Al Gore than Harrison Ford, right there in front of everyone. He puts his arm around her waist and grins coprophagically. He has baby's breath, always unnaturally sweet without gum or anything, even in the middle of the night, despite all the coffee he drinks, despite aging. She swells briefly with reluctant joy from his sudden bold sweetness until she looks out on the room, its wealth of happily bustling productive male bodies, its framed painting of a horse, presumably from some thrift store, its central good brown wooden table, a fridge off to the side with important messages clipped all over, and Noah, who looks like he's trying hard to stare at anything else…she looks back at Phil's smug face, mutters something she hopes sounds apologetic, gives a little wave the other way, and darts out the front door. How long her and Phil's relationship had been leading to this—in the sack, at stores when she was bored, at parties, and yet—at his mother's house, in pictures on Facebook, probably in Phil's head—absolutely not leading to this.

Outside there is a fog. Weird how fog is never in front of your face. How some things can be ubiquitous but only visible from a distance. It hangs and so does a smell, like cigarettes. When she and her roommate Elise cleaned their old apartment out in August two years ago it was so humid the piles of trash they threw away in the back alley made the whole block smell awful and there was nothing anyone could do about it. Boredom and consequences and longing creep all around like wraiths all the time. Stay out.

Chapter 3: Elvis Ray Sincere's Comprehensive List of His Own Fan Fiction

Spider-Man versus Les Assassins des Fauteuils Rollents from *Infinite Jest*: J. Jonah Jameson paints Spidey as beating up on the disabled, and Peter Parker furnishes the photos for it.

The Great Gazoo in a brawl with Cthulhu.

Oscar Wao in a swordfight with J. Alfred Prufrock over Daisy Buchanan. Daisy does not care about either man, but she is excited at the attention nonetheless.

Rabbit Angstrom and the aliens from Space Jam square off against Kenny Powers and the Harlem Globetrotters – in Calvinball.

Hazel Motes and Ignatius Reilly get into a fight online.

Medea meets Madea.

Slash: Holden Caulfield and Hannah Horvath.

Slash: Frasier Crane and Smaug.

Scully and Mulder accidentally kill Nick and Nora Charles, and have to figure out what to do with the bodies.

Yoshi does pot.

Walter White and Daniel Plainview making out.

Spider-Man versus clinical depression.

Spider-Man versus the recession.

Spider-Man versus lupus.

Remus Lupin versus lupus versus Uncle Remus.

Vladimir and Estragon get big into podcasting.

Garfield goes to the Interzone.

William S. Burroughs gets hooked on Unobtainium.

The Flintstones go to the Interzone—giant bugs and talking anuses work as construction equipment and staplers and say, "It's a living."

The Poppers from Peter Orner's *Love and Shame and Love* have a picnic with the Glass family. Everything goes great until the Wolfman shows up!

The Green Lantern versus the outside world.

Aquaman versus my former boss.

Frankenstein conquers my mom.

Tarzan kicks the shit out of the way I feel when I look into the blank space under "What I Do on A Typical Saturday Night" on dating profiles.

Swamp Thing defeats the smug, questioning look people give you during job interviews, as if to say, by giving you that look, "Oh, please explain further, crazy person," as if it's like that unreasonable to have had to take some time off work from 2007-2009 on account of all the emotional stress incurred and whatnot.

My Little Pony versus Night of the Lepus.

Night of the Lepus versus lupus.

James Bond enters a clinic for exhaustion and makes out with all the nurses.

Nicolas Cage's character in "Wild at Heart" finds that he can't finish reading a single book from his childhood without tearing up because he remembers how inconsequential the struggles, how unconditional the love.

Harry and the Hendersons learn to use the force.

FDR and Hitler settle World War II with a drinking contest. Churchill has to sit out because it would be unfair.

Bush and Saddam settle the Iraq War with a weed-smoking contest.

Hong Kong Phooey, number one super guy, can't stop dreaming about women mocking his genitals.

Animal and Miss Piggy find themselves really capable of having a mature and fulfilling relationship as platonic friends.

Pee-Wee Herman gets fired from Good Burger for repeatedly calling his coworker, Beatrice from the oeuvre of Dante, late at night and begging her to read a short story he wrote, after which Pee-Wee resorts to living in a fantasy world—a literal one!—populated by totally original characters, who ultimately teach Pee-Wee to embrace work and solitude and adulthood, no matter how painful they may seem. I think that one's my favorite.

Chapter 4: A Party, Condom Troubles, a Barfight, a Facebook Revelation, and the Unfortunate Fate of a Heroically-Named Hamster

Daniel and Trevor are having a rager at their place. Trevor is tall and mellow and morose and Daniel's mother once referred to him as "that boy who lounges and mutters cryptic things." Daniel is short and a little chubby and likes to wear blazers and jeans. Also: Jimmy's mother kicked him out of the house a month ago and he has been staying there on the couch ever since. The lights are low and Trevor has cleared some space in the living room/ kitchen/ dining area for people to dance. Trevor's laptop sits on a shelf connected to his big stereo and imposing brown speakers he got from his dad. There is a section of the wall where one night he and Daniel and Jimmy and Phil and Josie had all drawn this big mural together with felt pens, a universe of dicks and fedora-wearing whales and barfing gnomes and dancing skeletons and pizza. Jimmy had thrown a glass of water in his mother's face when she called him a "dilettante"—

which, he supposes, he actually is. Last month Jimmy tried to kiss Phil's girlfriend Josie in a bout of anger and confusion. Josie broke up with Phil later, and she has been in a party k-hole since, staying out just about every night, spending what seems to Jimmy like a ton of money at bars, and a couple times hooking up with Jimmy on that couch or in her tchotchke-adorned bedroom. She is supposed to be here tonight. Hardly anyone has even heard from Phil lately.

•

Josie and Elise get to the party about an hour after the invite said to and it is as raging as promised. A fog machine goes off in intrusive bursts—later someone will end up unplugging it because you can't see anything and people will bump into chairs and shit, and also the smell, like a dentist's office, just really overpowering. "They Live" plays on the TV and "Pony" by Ginuwine belches forth from these old speakers. Jimmy is doing what Josie would characterize as a somewhat mean, nonspecific imitation of what dancing is supposed to look like, swiveling his groin and flailing his elbows and sticking his tongue out and furrowing his brow. Josie thinks Jimmy, with his slouch and long straight black hair and same Garfield t-shirt he was wearing last time she saw him, would be almost comically handsome in a like Mediterranean way if not for his eyes being a little too close together. Josie has lost weight in the past month from breakup stress and hating-her-job stress but she still has a pretty big ass, which she is happy with. She also likes her lips, which always kind of poof out, and her tits are of the size where you can present them in an impressive way if you have the right bra, but they are also not too cumbersome.

The playlist moves from classic party hits to last-few-years Top 40-type stuff. Josie goes to hug Jimmy and he wriggles away and turns his face to the side. She takes a beer and swigs it with confidence and goes to do a different but equally mocking dance at Elise, hands up in the air like some children's performer, like nobody has ever hurt her feelings. Everything, as long as Josie has been aware of the world around her, has been a maze of espionage and code and dualistic self-promotion and double meanings and everyone feeling generally confused and frustrated with each other and with themselves. Everyone kidding or saying they're just kidding. Josie throws up her pale clay arms and doubles her pace.

.

But so anyways, later, here are Jimmy and Josie on the couch, everyone else has gone or is in their rooms, the fog is lifting, someone has knocked a bunch of books off the shelf and bottles and cans lie everywhere. How awful life's little victories can be, she thinks, how nauseating in their smallness. But Josie's got this. This is for her.

"Hit me inna face," she whispers. He winces and softly holds her ear.

"Put your hand on my neck." This is the first time she's tried this with him. He doesn't have it in him, she can tell, once she was walking with him and he tried to chase down a cat for like two blocks because it looked like something was wrong with its tail. He has cried to her about losing Chloe. He moves his hand now across her upper chest firmly but by no means roughly. She can smell the Hurricane on his breath. Apparently he is only sadistic in public. She slides off and makes an excuse about being tired, aligning herself next to him on the couch. There is barely room.

.

Phil wakes up every day at around 7:00 a.m. to the sound of calls from SubTron: Your Automated Substitute Teacher Request Service. He stays in bed ignoring the calls until noon, about a hundred calls. Sometimes he puts on The Smiths. He hasn't masturbated in a while. In retrospect, sex-wise, Josie always seemed like she wanted something more that she wasn't explicitly asking for. She was criminally good at Scrabble and would smirk in this adorable, mischievous way when she got a high score. She frequently put into motion ideas for daytrips to places like Dino Island, where this dude out in the country had built a bunch of wooden dinosaurs in the '70s. She made sandwiches for them to bring, and burned CDs. He had lost her by being so boring, and now he has spiraled into total, near-dead boringness. Every time the phone rings a stupid part of him thinks maybe it's her. When the SubTron calls stop he goes to his parents' place, where he watches '90s sitcoms on Totally: Your All '90s Sitcom Network until his parents make him sit down to dinner. This behavior is not self-flagellating so much as crying out for help from the only people who have ever helped him, but his parents don't seem to pick up on it. Phil's parents' place is a recent downgrade, a townhouse they bought when Phil's little sister went to college, and it's covered in pictures of Phil's parents' recent trips to Jamaica and to Las Vegas. The rugs and couch and chairs are all that gold and burgundy combo older bourgie types can't get enough of. If it doesn't remind them of their money and their wine it doesn't appeal to them. At dinner, Dad brags about being passive-aggressive to a woman in Demographics who had, "A hair across her ass." Mom says something about antioxidants. Dad asks what the new music is now. Dad's tennis elbow is getting better. Maybe this part is a little bit self-flagellating.

Tonight, Daniel and Trevor show up at Mom and Dad's. Shit, Phil thinks, the guys have found me out. What will I tell them I've been up to lately?

No, wait, he thinks—what a little scumbag I am! I've abandoned my friends. They miss me. Look at these guys. What a refreshing sight, even though Trevor has an ironic mullet now and it looks like Daniel has spilled something on his sweater!

Trevor says, "We're going to get Phil some pussy," to Phil's dad. Mom hoots. Dad says, "Well, shit, yeah." Daniel grins directly at Phil.

·

On his eighteenth birthday, Daniel's mother gave him the family minivan and bought herself a Jetta. Daniel is twenty-five now and still hasn't quite figured out how to drive the van in a remotely safe or sane way. He fucks with the music and whips his neck back constantly like some cartoon wolf to admire babes and he argues with Trevor and constantly swerves and misses turns. This van is a living terror, knifing through the suburban night with a collective mind. Trevor selects and pumps "Greatdayndamornin'/ Booty" by D'Angelo.

Phil says, "Daniel, driving with you remains the most soulful nightmare of all." The others laugh; Phil is back.

Trevor discusses his new job at a sandwich shop: "People come in and they're honestly bewildered. They say, 'I've lived in this neighborhood for thirty years. And y'all are chargin' seven dollars for a *sandwich?* And I'm a Ph.D. *candidate in Urban Planning* and I don't have a good answer for them."

"Yeah, but dude," Daniel replies, "garlic aioli."

•

The walls of the bar, "H.W. Sportz's," are yellow like those of an elementary school, or a room that might drive a literary character to post-partum insanity. There are TVs in most corners of the walls playing March Madness. The bartenders wear ref uniforms. After two Blue Moons Phil is swimming on the surface of life, tipsy for the first time in a couple weeks. All around it seems like everyone else's life is a beer commercial.

Phil asks how Jimmy's been. Trevor stares sidelong at Daniel until Daniel just starts shouting along to the song playing overhead, something about having a good time tonight.

Now Trevor is goading Phil to go talk to this Asian girl—how bold we are on our friends' behalves—and Phil is actually considering it. Why shouldn't he talk to her? She is alone and has great bangs and is wobbling one elbow around in a cute way to the rhythm of the song playing. Phil thinks: I can tell a roomful of high school kids, towering, sweating, horny mutants, to please be quiet and take out their copies of whatever. I can tell Daniel he doesn't know shit about shit, when that is the case. I am capable of acting on my desires.

Josie used to get so worried about finances she'd cry into Phil's armpit and sort of burrow into it like a cat might. Before they started dating, Josie used to brag about sleeping with some older guy named Charles Buddy who allegedly had a big penis and was generally so huge of a guy he could just throw her all around the bedroom, and who wanted to marry her. Somehow Phil had convinced her of his own neediness, of the demanding nature of his presence. As he had spent his childhood doing to his mother, Phil had insisted, "I am here," and Josie had had to attend to him.

Phil gets up and walks towards the girl without looking to see how Daniel and Trevor react. It turns out the girl's name is Natalie and she is Cambodian. In the seventies, Phil knows, Pol Pot's dictatorship led to the deaths of a substantial amount of the population of Cambodia, after the United States invaded completely unnecessarily and refused to aid them once the war was over. Phil's whiteness and his American-ness are just another part of what he hates about himself, and for that reason he watches a lot of documentaries about Vietnam by himself. He avoids the subject.

It turns out Phil and Natalie have been to a number of the same concerts in the past year, and Natalie also thinks AMC's "Breaking Bad" is *amazing, and* she agrees with Phil that this place is a "bit much!" Phil ignores a text from Trevor and

ends up waving goodbye to them after another
hour or so, and then Phil and Natalie are out in the
parking lot, up against her car, and the humiliating
thoughts which occupy Phil's mind most of the
time—*my skin looks like pizza dough, my breath is
probably weird from the coffee I drank earlier, I
blew it with Josie forever, and I will never find
someone as cool as her*—disappear with the guilt—
*what am I doing with my education? I'm
squandering privileges people on the other side of
the world only dream about just to be one of those
disgusting people you see making out in semi-
public*—as he pushes his face up against hers, which
seems to sparkle, and she scrunches her nose up
and giggles and oh God the sky—

Phil admires the light pink walls of Natalie's
room. She has a canopy bed and there is a painting
of a horse on the wall. ("Are you an equestrian?"
"No, Cambodian.") Natalie is nineteen and goes to
Bluffberg Tech. She used her sister's ID to get in to
H.W. Sportz's. She wants to be a graphic designer.
Her parents are out of town. She gives Phil all this
information in response to questions he's asking
with an increasingly weirded-out tone. She kisses his
neck and pulls on his shirt and sits on the bed. They
make out until Phil is pushing his whole body
against her on top of the bed, and she is grabbing at
his groin. His self-esteem is like through the roof at
this point. The lights stay on this whole time. She

fumbles for a little drawer to the side of the head of the bed and opens the drawer and takes out a condom, one of those numbers with the big shiny wrapper like they give away at Planned Parenthood or on college campuses during Sexual Health Awareness Month—a brand he'd almost forgotten about. His hands shake pitifully as he tries to pry open the packaging, which is both hard and kind of slippery, and to maintain an erection at this point he has to keep grinding up against her leg. He finally rips the wrapper apart but swings back too hard and punches himself in the mouth. She asks if he's okay and he chuckles yeah, then begins scrutinizing the piece of latex for the right place to pinch so there's no air bubbles. As always, he is unsatisfied with his own pinching ability, he has the same trouble tying ribbons on presents, but decides to make do before it's too late. But it's not the same anymore; his brief self-esteem high is now tinged with frustration and self-doubt and, of course, guilt. She doesn't seem to notice. She says, "You are so soulful, you know that? You are like such a soulful guy." His confidence again builds as he pushes her back and forth and she smiles that candy smile. He is an oil rig, he is a conquistador, Columbus, colonizing her nation for golden pride, building his empire. Wait, Columbus? No, he thinks, this is all wrong. This is terrible. I am terrible and everything I represent is terrible.

"I can't do this. I'm sorry. It was lovely meeting you." Phil stands and Natalie sits up, undies still around her ankles, face slack in apparent shock. He is out the door so fast he can barely hear the vulgar, incredulous expression she shouts from her room. She'll see one day: we are all heroes for putting up with ourselves all the time.

·

Josie's phone rings that morning and she wakes up on the couch with Jimmy's arm in her face. It's Katelyn Studebaker from work, who asks Josie where she is.

"What? I wasn't scheduled today."

"You're on the schedule and you have to get down here. It's a disaster."

Josie swings her feet over the edge and does a hunched-over sit for a couple minutes, then starts walking from Trevor and Daniel's over to MyPetResource. Jimmy doesn't get up. Katelyn was a little gleeful in relaying the message to Josie that she had fucked up, Josie thinks. Katelyn has been jealous of Josie ever since she got promoted. When the promotions got handed down, Katelyn got all, "I am *so happy for you*," but frowning. And then moped around the rest of the day. When someone asks who the manager is, Katelyn always takes a second to pretend to remember, and then Josie has to jump in. Every time. Katelyn takes twenty, twenty-one minute breaks instead of fifteen-minute breaks, which is the amount you're supposed to take, but when Josie brought that up to the other managers at the meeting last week, they were all like, Uhh, we don't know about that. Katelyn Studebaker—wait, whatever. At Apartheid, people would literally just disappear and never come back. People would have sex in the stock room.

.

It is a disaster though. Dogs are whining, cats are mewling, some animals have peed and pooped in their cages and it smells bad, some woman is yelling about how she needed cat food two hours ago...the really disturbing thing is that a hamster, Batman, has gnawed the face off his cage-mate, Robin. Robin stands motionless but keeps breathing, sort of wheezing through his fucked-up bald face. Batman gazes off innocently, blood spattered all over his cute little nose. It's hard to say whether or not either one realizes something life-altering has just happened to both of them. Josie gasps, but then settles down and says, "Okay, but three hours? That's not because I was three hours late. He got that hungry in three hours?"

"Yes!" Katelyn practically yells.

"That's a fucking cannibal hamster, man."

"Oh, for Christ's sake!"

.

"Of course, I cried in the bathroom for forty-five minutes after, though..." Josie is back in Daniel and

Trevor's living room/ kitchen/ dining room, on the couch with Jimmy, passing a bong back and forth. It's pretty late.

"You have the easiest job in the world," Jimmy mutters.

"Fuck *you*, I had to flush this faceless hamster down the toilet, alive! And I had to clean the blood off the other one's *face!*" She is close to tears again now.

"Can't believe you didn't get fired." Jimmy opens his laptop and Daniel and Trevor burst in all excited.

"Phil is totally fucking some bitch right—oh." Daniel sees Josie. Josie coughs.

"You guys," Jimmy says. "You guys, guys, guys, shut up a minute, guys. Shut the fuck up a minute."

"What's Phil doing?" Josie says.

"Chloe's getting married," Jimmy says.

No one says anything.

"According to Facebook." Jimmy's breath is hard and fast. "She's engaged. Some guy I've never heard of. Some guy in France she's never mentioned." His chest looks more sunken than is even possible. His eyes are popping and his jaw is jutting out. "Or maybe she has mentioned him. I don't know."

Almost immediately and without a word, the four proceed to the bar directly under the apartment. Outside, a big guy in a red sweatshirt with a bored look and a goatee checks everyone's

IDs. Josie demands four shots of whiskey and they take the shots. Daniel and Trevor see this guy Prentice, a white guy with dreadlocks who always talks about starting a record label. Like he's always going on about some uncle who lives in Jamaica who has a recording studio? Like, talk about something else sometime, man. She doesn't know why Daniel and Trevor like him so much. Josie orders another shot.

"That was last call, did you *not hear?*"

The bartender has a skinny face and a skinny tie, and something about his tone makes her snap. Like he's any better than any of us college-educated people working horrible jobs and having to talk to each other. Like he thinks he's the first one ever for whom this life was not enough.

"What's your problem? Seriously, what is wrong with you?" she says. He sneers and laughs and starts to turn the other way when she grabs his tie and pulls hard. She is Nat Turner, she is the Black Panthers, Israel, the Viet Cong, the Afghani insurgency. The oaf from out front grabs her from behind off the barstool. She wraps her legs tight around it, managing to take it with her for several of the bouncer's large steps. It falls down and everyone looks around and now she is kicking her legs. The ID-checker flings her onto the sidewalk like the time she fell off that tractor as a child only much more aggressive and some instinct tells her to put her hands out to protect her face but then, fuck, the searing pain in her hands, and the main emotion she feels is *disbelief* at how much actual pain she is in, and just before she blacks out she hears Jimmy and the bouncer shouting at each other and just feels embarrassed for both of them, and she sees a waning orange streetlight above, and she thinks of her mother on the town council, and of Phil.

·

Monday night Josie is clicking aimlessly on her laptop when her phone rings and it's Phil.

"I was just calling because I thought you'd appreciate this: I was drinking coffee and I put it on the window ledge by my chair. I forgot the coffee was there after, like, a second, and spilled it all over myself. I haven't even cleaned it up yet, my first instinct was to tell you about it."

She laughs. "I do appreciate that. It wasn't hot, was it?"

"No, just lukewarm."

They talk for another few minutes and he says he has to go. Outside, through a parting of curtains, she can see cars pushing up hills, little red ants carrying ten times their weight in adult sadness and pride. Her arm is in a sling, but she decides not to tell him about that, for now.

Chapter 5: We Went to Las Vegas And It Was Mostly Just Sad

By Daniel Fairchild, Zazzpop staff
12/3/2011, 8:15 a.m.

We wanted to go to Vegas. It was summer, we both had enough time off from work, and we'd never been. In high school, we both read *Fear and Loathing in Las Vegas* and watched the movie and quoted it and bought a poster and framed our infantile adventures—going the next town over and losing our way, buying lots of convenience store junk food—in Raoul Duke terminology.

We hadn't been yet because Vegas is, by all accounts, stupid. Even in high school we knew the difference between the tourist trap and Thompson's subversive descriptions of his alter-ego's debauchery. Still, the city holds a promise: from "The Hangover" to Vegas's current ad slogan, "What Happens in Vegas Stays in Vegas," the place seemed to us a Disneyland of potential guilt. It had to be! When Trevor proposed the trip, his words weighed heavily with the excitement and terror of history. You told someone, my dad for instance, you were going to Vegas and the reaction was invariably a lively and cautious and vicarious, "*Ooh!* You guys are gonna get yourselves in *trou-ble!*" We went for the reason anyone goes: to say we went.

We bought fruit snacks and pretzels and grapes and twelve bottle waters wrapped in plastic. We blasted Slayer and Cannibal Corpse like Odysseus giving the finger to Poseidon before setting off on his journey. We drove through Kentucky and Missouri and Kansas and Colorado and Utah and stayed in hotels and smoked weed and watched Letterman. Fields and slaughterhouses and stores full of Native American-y shit and sunglasses and voluptuous rivers and finally the ominous orange city on the hill: total entertainment.

Being in Las Vegas is like being in Times Square in an alternate universe where different, more insipid things are popular. Everything that looms over you is an ad for some big deal of a musical production or stage show you've never heard of, I hope: there's "Menopause: The Musical" (a menstrual show!); several variations on revues in which women take off some, but not a significant amount of, their clothes while singing…one show is pirate-themed; some all-male variations of same thing, but I don't think the men have to sing; "Greg London's Impressions that ROCK," in which a man apparently imitates a heavily-tanned Ozzy Osbourne, a heavily-tanned one of the guys from ZZ

Top, a heavily-tanned Elvis... An old woman interviewed for a commercial playing on a screen above us in a casino at one point praised Greg London as "better than Sammy Davis." There's naked Cirque du Soleil, Beatles Cirque du Soleil, Michael Jackson Cirque du Soleil, and regular Cirque du Soleil. One can go on a bus tour of great Mafia hits.

If Vegas is a Mecca for devout gamblers, those who people-watch religiously should consider it as well. First, leaving the hotel, we encountered six or seven similarly stout, middle-aged people of Native American descent draped in orange vests handing out literature containing information on how to procure the services of prostitutes. These pamphlets also described the escorts' various attributes as if the women were cats you could adopt: "feisty," "perfect for couples," "may bite." We saw so many relationships so much less honest than the classic hooker-john relationship, so many ringed, fat, hairy hands on so many tiny black lacey waists. I started to panic. I couldn't help but envision the foreplay these couples must have! Nothing like the sincere, fragile experiences I'd enjoyed with Alice and Claire, that tender cute sadness, taking the shirt off a girl you feel very nervous around, whose opinions you agree with and are interested in, but more like pretending to be the boss of some woman's negligee because you bought it. Sexual batting cages. It made me think: Christ, I better get on my fucking bike once in a while, stop going to Taco Bell, start approaching girls on the bus or whatever or I'll be forced into a life of the latter type of sex and forever miss out on the former.

Not that I'll ever have the kind of money these third-wife-havers have. But I can all too clearly see myself in an insincere relationship with someone I can't relate to, one day. Vegas is so overwhelming in this way, you don't even have to drink that much or spend a lot of money or do anything irresponsible in order to feel guilty and incapacitated.

We walked past a big sports gambling area with a wall of TV screens set to different games and a crowd betting on the games. An elderly man sat in a chair watching one of the games intently while his wife, holding his hand, slept. What Tolstoy said about unhappy families is not entirely true in tourist attractions. Every unhappy family is, in fact, similarly overweight and pale and whiny in vocal timbre. The fathers—serious brown mustaches, XL polo shirts—all have looks of resolve in their eyes. The mothers manifest former creative knacks through insults and pointless questions directed at no one. Stepmoms with drinks as tall as kids, long plastic containers of slushy booze with straws for their lip-lined mouths. The children are amorphous and rightly confused and upset. I'm all for golden calves and Sodom and Gomorrah, but maybe don't drag your kids there, especially when it's actually boring.

Most stereotypical tourists are probably uncomfortable in normal society. Only in having the excuse of, "Hey, I'm a tourist, I'm not from around here!" can they be free to wear lanyards and walk slowly in zigzags and have very private arguments in public while eating ice cream.

One particular dad, I guess slightly drunk—cargo shorts, fanny pack, skinny, loud, close-cropped graying beard—walked in front of us on the strip for a long time. He walked with his wife and two preteen kids, a boy and a girl, but was bonding with another dad he'd just met and monologuizing:

"Tell ya, the ancient Greeks would send their babies to a cliff to fend for themselves! Kids who came back got to live another day! Call that thinnin' out the herd!" Seismic dad-laughs. "Nowadays you gotta keep your kids 'til they're twenty, twenty-five, thirty!" You can imagine the faces his kids were making.

A guy in a devil costume, alone. People smoking cigars. Bachelor and bachelorette parties walking with the same grim determination as those dads. In Vegas, I felt the same sadness as when one of my parents would give me something I didn't like or want for Christmas: disappointment mixed with pity (and—I admit!—just a little contempt) for the older generation, and a little shame for being such an ingrate myself, although my parents would never have actually articulated such feelings towards me. My natural defense of laughing at people who seem ridiculous broke down, because everyone was ridiculous in a profoundly poignant way, myself included. I actually began to feel concern at my own inability to feel schadenfreude. A very important psychological mechanism of mine had stopped working!

Trevor went to the bathroom and came back to report, "Two delightful things about that bathroom: one, every stall above it had a picture of a woman looking down at you with an impressed, lustful look—one had a ruler out; two, a man was just sitting down on the floor crying in that bathroom."

When we were kids we would go around looking for rare and valuable items, like gold and fossils, convinced we would find something just in the ground. The biggest discovery came one day when Trevor proclaimed that, because of the way it sparkled in the late-August Virginia sun, clearly every inch of the entire road everywhere across America was made of tiny expensive diamonds. Recently, I've begun to feel like the opposite is true: that everything we stand on is worthless and false.

Trevor sat down and took a bite of his Sbarro pizza. "So what do we do, dude? Just give up?"

"I think we should at least get a drink first."

"No, I mean, in life. Do we just become the kind of people who go to Vegas?"

"Naw, man. Your academic stuff is gonna go great, I have faith in my writing—"

"But I feel sleazy already, right?"

"Well what's the worst that can happen? We become lame?"

"We become the kind of people you and I would make fun of here."

"Right. Or the kind of people who make me wanna fucking cry, here."

"Like we are actually at a precipice in our lives right now, where we could just decide to become sad-ass people."

"But anyone could do that at any time."

"But *we* could do it without even changing or making any decisions."

Another memory: when my sister and I were I guess like nine and ten, my mother took us to this place, The Rainforest Café, which was a restaurant with animatronic gorillas and crocodiles and jaguars, plus the occasional real tropical fish and birds. Afterwards, my mother was furious for reasons that I, at the time, didn't understand. She muttered something about "fifty dollars...in a fake rainforest." I guess she felt surrounded by artifice all the time, like when she was growing up in the sixties and seventies, things were going to get all-natural and organic, and it never happened, and so the plastic animals really set her off. She probably at one point thought her life would have some real adventure in it.

And don't tell me the real adventure in life is raising your kids and having experiences with them and seeing them grow up, because The Rainforest Café fucking sucks.

We went to this bar where an actual piano man was singing and playing classic rock hits on one of those electronic pianos made to look like a baby grand. The pianist was a light-skinned African-American guy with crazy muscles, a shaved head, and a tan t-shirt with a splattery design all over it. He was just going to town on "Free Fallin'," which is maybe my least favorite song of all time. This family was seated at a table near the piano: husband and wife around the same age, him in all khaki, almost safari-looking clothes, mom plump and radiant, older daughter serious and approachably good-looking, younger daughter dolled up in a sleeveless crimson dress, drinking a Sea Breeze and undulating her shoulders and neck to the music in a way that was exuberant, almost sexual, yet still respectful of her parents' presence. We would later learn it was her 21st birthday. She loves Jesus, and horses too.

"I'm saying," Trevor continued, "we're already there. We're being kind of lame. Not enjoying ourselves. We've already gotten there! Or okay, lemme put it this way: that man who was in front of us earlier, talking loudly about the ancient Greeks and shit. King Spartacus there."

"Uh-huh."

"You marry that guy's daughter."

"I marry King Spartacus's daughter?"

"Correct. You marry his daughter, she's perfect, she's great. Absolute best-case scenario, you've managed to avoid him like three times in a row. Thanksgiving, Christmas, somebody's in the hospital."

"Sure."

"So now you can't really get out of it, you really have to spend summer vacation with King Spartacus, and he wants to take the kids to see the Hoover Dam. Possibly to dangle them over the edge and invoke the terror of his beloved ancient Greeks. And you say, okay, honey, but only if you and I can go to Vegas. Then—"

"Fuck!"

"Then not only are you in Vegas, but it's your fault you're in Vegas."

"That is compelling."

"And you realize Vegas, for as much as we're mocking and hating it now, will actually be a high point for you in the context of the past few years where you're just yelling and sending emails and watching Meryl Streep movies and just walking around your house, because, my God, there's a store that sells M&M's shit! Gumball machines and pillows! And a piano player singing 'Hey Jude!' Or whatever our generation's equivalent of that will be. 'Niggaz in Paris,' or 'That's My Bitch.'"

"'Hey Jude' is really such a classic dick dad move. Like, 'Your mother and I don't love each other anymore, but *I'm in the Beatles*, and my boy Paul wrote this song for you...'"

"Y'know what the only happy thing about this place is? The waitress still sings along."

It was true. The woman—lean, late thirties maybe, black pantsuit, big frizzy black hair, was "*naaa*-na-na-nana-na-naaa"-ing for no one but herself as she bussed tables, picked up checks, grabbed another Sea Breeze for the birthday girl, who was now doing a corny lasso motion at us to get us to come dance, which is, of course, objectively the cutest fucking thing a human person can do, and of course we shrug and get up and dance. Of course.

Chapter 6: The View

From the backseat, Phil can see the shadow of
Ellis Grand—green-black like a bruise—as he
hunches over the maroon steering wheel of his '98
Volvo station wagon and constantly shifts back and
forth in his seat, his form illuminated in the night
whenever someone drives by. When Mr. Grand had
picked them up, Phil had observed the man looking
the same as ever: Hawaiian shirt with a Chinese
dragon across it, like they sell at Kohl's, clearly
hiding a tremendous beer belly, bright blue jeans
frayed and stringy in parts, and flip-flops. Hair
shoulder-length and wavy and auburn, like that of
the male porn star who hunts milves when he
started getting old and fat and they replaced him. A
perfect mustache—probably the least embarrassing
part about him—was a sunburned, innocent cat
asleep upon a perpetual frown. Eyes that always
looked a little frightened and confused, now hidden
by aviators. Josie, by her own admission, wanted to
bring Phil along because she hasn't told her father
they've broken up yet, and he likes Phil. That and
she can't stand to spend time with the man, for

reasons he's now illustrating by ranting over the live Ramones cassette tape playing, sounding almost exactly like that one Lou Reed live album where he talks over every song.

"That's why I never liked politics to begin with. I was never political, kids. But when Josie hooked up the Internet for me, it was like I became *awake*. You know what I mean? Like in that movie, *The Matrix*, when Christopher Reeves *[sic]* becomes finally aware of what's going on around him, how it's all fake and made by computers?"

"This guy, Mister *Obama*—" his voice develops a sarcastic tone, and Phil can see he's taken both hands off the steering wheel for long enough to wave them like jazz hands, "Mister *Fabulous*, President *Obama*, everyone *loves* him so much. Turns out he's instituted this *national healthcare* policy? Where they make you *buy healthcare?* They say we're a nation of doctors and lawyers now, well when they fire all the doctors, where does that leave us? Heh. And people say he's actually *not* against America. You know all of Capitol Hill, the hill, the actual hill, is an underground bunker, right? It's a known fact."

Josie has flipped around and is looking wide-eyed at Phil in alarm and amazement. Those eyes, like cream cheese, like swimming outside in perfect weather. Take me from my bed in your warm light and toy with me like aliens.

"It's this damn sense of entitlement in this country," Mr. Grand continues. "Like those kids on American Idol who can't sing worth a damn and no one's ever told them otherwise. They're the ones who'd give it all up to not have to pay their insurance. They would sell us all out for a free ride."

The cover of the new issue of Swamp Thing says, "IN THE HEART OF THE ROT...EVEN LOVE DIES!"

They get to the top of a hill and Phil can see the moon clearly from the window, can see the mountains and valleys glowing wildly, lonely, clamoring for attention, and he looks out at the city, the financial district hanging back ready to leap into violence at any minute. Flickering red lights of the past, of the South, of coal. God loves the city more than anywhere else, and don't they know it. He looks at the sky and across the river to all the buildings and their lights and cars and down, finally, to his fat legs in corduroy pants and tries to think the thing everyone always thinks when confronted by such discord in size and distance but he can't. He can't help but feel like it's all the same size.

Chapter 7: Now

Now it's December 1984, and Ellis is at what is, and will remain, the greatest party he has ever been to or will ever go to. He is in a room off to the side with three other people smoking and playing the new Tom Waits, talking loudly over each about the influence of Brecht but really it is unlike anything they have ever heard, sweet and junky and coarse and sad and brassy, bellowing and clattering all around the room like a tiny pack of jaunty little demons. Now a girl with giant brown eyes named Sandra or Heather is offering him LSD, which is kind of a passé drug at this point, but is Ellis a drug snob? No, he is not! Now it is kicking in and everything is crawling. Heather or Sandra and her brown shoulders pulsing. Ellis talks about his childhood ("Privileged but also essentially deprived, if you know what I mean.") and his ex-girlfriend ("And that was when I realized she was just a kid, you know what I mean? Just a *baby*.") and about Kerouac and Bukowski and *Five Easy Pieces*. He feels often like a reverse Dorothy, stumbling backwards through black-and-white bummer after bummer, but tonight he is not just watching

himself talk like an idiot and assert himself over
and over in horror like usual, he is okay being
around himself, in part because of how generous
and considerate everyone else seems to be about
listening to his opinions, in part because of this girl
and her eyes and her shoulders waving all around
him, Heather, Sandra, and also because this night is,
he is sure, the best of what Bluffberg, VA, has to
offer: rugs, and humans, and bongs, and talk, and
yellow light, and swimming around in it *while also
appearing smart* to everyone around him, somehow.

Out in the street there is rain.

Also at this party: a guy with red curly hair who
keeps yelling about Reagan, a punk rocker who
looks way too old, a dame who writes for the *Village
Voice*, a man in a Santa outfit who came in with two
chicks and is only talking to them, someone who
introduced himself to Ellis as "The Scientist."
Someone puts Mingus on and Ellis might, right
now, in December 1984, admit to you that it is not
the fantastic blazing beat or the way the saxes all
rush in like a tidal wave that appeals to him but in
fact the *idea* of Charles Mingus, the fact they put
the record on, and that he knows what it is, and like
that. Knowing that, even saying it maybe, but still
not hating himself for it, not seeing everything as
this big darkness, this wild black mass of unfairness
tonight. Heather or Cindy or Sandra (or perhaps,
Ellis thinks, she is all three of these people at once?

How delightful!) asks, Did it kick in? And Ellis stumbles, trying to think of something cool to say, and her laughter and eye contact are a net into which he safely falls. The old punk rocker is now making out with the *Voice* chick. He's got his hand on her lower back and is trying to touch as much of her ass with his palm as possible. It's a beautiful phenomenon to watch, like the time-lapsed creation of caves. Between this and Mingus's aggressive tides, Ellis feels he can see the entirety of geological history in this room.

Someone has made burgers. There is lemonade and sangria and burned pot brownies and Pabst Blue Ribbon. Ellis is just fascinated right now by the absence of that feeling he always gets in social situations, like hands pulling inside of his ribcage and filling it with a suffocating coolness. He is bursting, pushing the coolness out of him. Often he just wants to fall and keep falling until he stops, or to be hit by some kind of truck, but now he does not. Sometimes he wants his lungs to collapse, sometimes he wishes someone would set him on fire, sometimes he thinks, Beat the shit out of me, anyone, please, extinguish my desire, my constant foolish loudmouthed wanting. But not now, not tonight.

Now Lou Reed is at this party. His hair is yellow now and he is just like in the interviews: aloof and irreverent. Ellis can't hear him—what is he saying?

You can just see his sunglasses and his chimp-like mouth, that just barely opens when he talks. They say he pretty much does his own weight in heroin every day now. He played at the Diamond Room Wednesday night.

Lou Reed will get Cindra or Saundy to go to a hotel with him and step on his face for an hour, allegedly. Soon Ellis will re-watch that pickup artist video, that he secretly has—*sssshhhh!*—one last time and go talk to the girl in the cool yellow leather jacket who hangs around the diner he goes to every day to write poetry. He will meet and fuck that diner girl and he will go and write and write and become famous, he believes. A famous degenerate poet with her by his side. Or whoever else by his side. Or just tons of exciting one-night stands, so he can write about how "sad" it all is. He doesn't think about the blackness that is coming for him. He thinks: if I'm not depressed now, maybe things aren't as bad as they seem with, y'know, inflation, and deforestation... It'll be a new year soon. There will be plenty of time. Because what matters to Ellis is *now*. Because he is so sure, in this little green and yellow room with Mingus playing and fucking Lou fucking Reed coolly responding to things just beyond the door (and who does Lou Reed even know here? Santa?), and with the burgers and huge eyes and everything shimmering just a little bit, that this is how it will always be: how

America will be, what we'll all be doing. Lazing and analyzing and succeeding and being sensuous and potentially famous *all the time*. And it will always be like this. It will always be like this. It will always be like this. It will always be like this. It will always be like this. It

Chapter 8: Baby Girl

Caroline from the diner window on the street from behind, her tiny legs in tight, deep-violet dungarees marching emphatically under her yellow leather jacket, on the back of which she has stitched the words "BABY GIRL." A gray sky. Caroline coming towards you, hands perpetually stuffed in the side pockets of her jacket, hair a '50s-style orange pillar. Her approaching form, an armless, vertical tide.

Ellis Grand is several years out of college and unemployed, in what he will later refer to as his "Kerouac days." He borrows money from his old man and goes down to the Third Street Diner every morning and tries to write, and every morning she is there smoking cigarettes and laughing with her friends, some of whom are Afro-Americans, who, to Ellis, seem like visitors from a sooty, clamorous jungle planet, but with whom she seems to interact effortlessly.

Don't tell anyone, but Ellis at one point not long before this ordered from the back of an issue of Superman (Crisis on Infinite Earths!) one of those How-to-Seduce-Women tapes. In it, a man named

Sex Dave, who wore enormous glasses and whose fat face was terrifyingly incongruous to the muscular torso he showed off via tiny polo shirts, leaped through all these impressive star- or heart-shaped transitional wipes as he taught Ellis how to go over to Caroline's table one of the days she was by herself, speak in a commanding voice, make unceasing eye contact, get her name and use it repeatedly while addressing her; how to subtly command her to give him her number rather than just asking for it like some chump might, pick the movie, *Friday the 13th: A New Beginning. If the memory still haunts you, you're not alone.* Bloodshed, Sex Dave assures us, makes chicks horny even though they don't realize it.

Caroline, amused by Ellis's transparent feigned confidence, goes with him to *Friday the 13th* and later to see The Butthole Surfers, where someone vomits on her shoes, and she has him over to drink tequila and to listen to *Rain Dogs* and to talk, with increasing feverish boldness and increasingly confessional subtext about John Waters and about *Tropic of Cancer.* She gets close to him on her couch, this dark orange affair. They talk about their parents (Ellis: supportive but neurotic; Caroline: out of the picture, basically) and what high school was like for them (humiliating; brutally humiliating) and do they believe in God (kind of; kind of). Her apartment's walls are dark green and everything is lit at about waist level. His parent's place is vast and white like church. His parents both go out of town frequently but she meets his mother once. She takes them out for dinner and sends her foie gras back twice and spends most of the dinner conversation muttering about it, about how she usually likes this place, and nagging Ellis to go to the dentist. Back then, Ellis used to wear these cowboy boots.

So when Caroline misses her period for two straight weeks, she takes the bus out to the suburbs to see him, this funny, hirsute, cowboy-boot-wearing man who has been fumbling and jiving his way into her womb. When she breaks the news Ellis stands up, massages his nascent writerly beard with his right hand for several seconds and excuses himself to go smoke one of his Pall Malls. She knows immediately by this gesture, and by his face's sudden paleness, that he is not thinking of birth but of the silent end of his life of spending hours at the diner every day, of going and getting hammered in the city with her, of his regular use of psychotropic mushrooms, possibly even the death of his ambitions as the next Bukowski. She knows this even before she hears the engine of his VW Rabbit start.

Caroline stands up in Ellis's parents' white kitchen, and the sun is shining oppressively through the bay windows behind her. She looks at her arms, how the light reflects off them. She looks at the handsome brown liquor cabinet and the sparkling living room chandelier and listens to the droning Frigidaire, and of course thinks of smashing it all, of burning it all, robbing a bank and stealing a car and skipping town, but only briefly. Reasoned, measured points begin to form in her floating head: that she wants to have a baby, never realized it before but desperately wants to hold an infant and nurse it and teach it to walk. That the wanting of the thing is enough. Whether it's a good idea doesn't matter because wanting shapes your life, can shape a life that is currently formless, a life that revolves around eating diner food and working at a shoe store and fucking and drinking tequila and drinking coffee and being a hipster, which is no kind of life at all, not really, and things like wanting and urgency and necessity and desperation can be inherently redeeming. Can shape your life, and her life is overdue for being shaped. She wants with equal desperation for Ellis to be a good person. She wants him to know that actions have consequences. She wants him to *know her.* She lets the front door of the house hang open as she leaves. She catches the bus.

Ellis's car runs out of gas just outside of town, on the side of the highway, marsh all around. He spends several hours trying to hitchhike, but this is the '80s, nobody picks up hitchhikers anymore. He walks a mile on the side of the road to get a tank of gas and when he fills the Rabbit up, he drives it to the diner, its status for him as a warm haven of normalcy and freedom is apparently even stronger than its connection to Caroline. But she is there, waiting for him, and over the blare of Springsteen she corners and berates and browbeats Ellis for the sake of the livelihood of the baby she has already half-seriously decided to name after a Clint Eastwood character whether it's a boy or a girl. She says, "Look, I get it. I totally get it." Like she's Jimmy Carter. He says, "I guess, the only thing I'm really afraid of is the immensity of feelings I have for you." Which she, sort of out of emotional necessity, chooses to believe.

The idea of marriage has never appealed to Caroline, but the idea of her own wedding does. Figuring out what wine and food to get on a limited budget, inviting all her girls, and at least one dude to make jealous, picking out the songs ("Sweetheart" by Suicide for her and Ellis's dance, "Beat It" for when everyone else joins in.) She likes controlling things like that, setting scenes. The only thing that pisses her off is having to take her shoes off during the service, at the insistence of Dennis Swain, Ellis's ordained-minister acquaintance who officiates the ceremony, and who also owns the artists' colony she and Ellis will soon be moving into. Even Ellis's mother, who came off as insanely controlling the one other time Caroline had met her, manages to leave the creative aspects alone, perhaps because the circumstances are so freaky in the first place, and maybe because the Grands are contributing so little of their, apparently, pretty substantial wealth to the ceremony.

Caroline's father is dead, drove into the wall of a credit union hammered one night when Caroline was seventeen. Caroline sends an RSVP to her mother, who Caroline has not spoken to since college. She never responds.

After the wedding, Caroline and Ellis move to Swain's artists' colony, which is a fixed-up five-bedroom house in a part of town where a shoe factory closed down five years ago, and which has since become incredibly dangerous. A news report comes out about people in the area getting hooked on this new, cheap type of cocaine that's laced with like laundry detergent? You hear gunshots just about every night, and whole packs of abandoned, starving pit bulls roam around the neighborhood. You hear about them attacking people and you hear snarling and growling late at night, and you see the occasional lone pit—gray, scraggly, wounded all over—making the kind of unpleasant face you'd never thought you'd see on a dog...

Ellis writes all day. Working on a novel. He paces and drinks whiskey and goes out back and smokes Pall Malls, despite smoking being against house rules. The novel is about a hard-drinking poet trying to survive the fascist Reagan era, escaping his nagging cunt wife, and hitting the road, where he encounters violent Negroes, faggots, prostitutes, and hillbillies, but ultimately discovers the real meaning of freedom.

Caroline has long since lost interest in any work related to her college major, political science, and, having been a consistent member of the service industry for years now, feels only a small pain in joining the three other female residents in working to keep the house and manage groceries—the utility feels good, although the sexism doesn't.

The house's rules are written on a white piece of paper in magic marker and posted on the house's front door:

1. NO CORDLESS PHONES INSIDE THE HOUSE. THOSE THINGS R FOR YUPPIES!

2. THERE IS NO TELEVISION INSIDE THIS HOUSE, NOR WILL THERE EVER BE.

3. ALL FOOD EATEN INSIDE IS TO BE PREPARED INSIDE. GOING OUT TO EAT IS EXPRESSLY FROWNED UPON.

Despite the arbitrary rigidity of these rules, Caroline does not begin to feel uncomfortable with the artists' colony environment until Swain's weekly meetings commence, during which everyone else sits rapt as Swain rants against western medicine, the UN, and MSG. He asks vague rhetorical questions like, "Who holds all the power?" and no matter how any of the audience members tailor their responses to sound like something he wants to hear, the answers are always wrong. He always takes those opportunities to show how "brainwashed" everybody is. His mannerisms—sniffing, clapping, and shouting at random intervals—start to betray an escalating coke habit, and at least four female members of the artists' colony at some point, while doing dishes, admit to Caroline they have slept him, all volunteering the information in this same coy, half-boastful way, the same slight shrug and glint in their eyes, as if they have all practiced saying it that way together. Caroline maybe feels slightly disappointed that he never comes on to her, and figures it is only because she is so huge at this point.

Caroline feels hesitant about the natural birth everyone insists she have within the confines of the artists' colony, but reasons that every woman throughout history has done it until relatively recently—isn't she as tough as them? And does anyone really have a right to complain about not being drugged for an experience? Childbirth, it turns out, feels exactly the way it looks: like being eviscerated, exploding like a you-sized zit, entering a spherical force field of huge cruel pink pain that belongs only to you, a pain which rolls and collects more of itself like kids building a snowman, such that she actually hallucinates, sees sinister gray faces like daguerreotypes out of the corner of her eye, an emergency, until everything spills horribly, gloriously out of her like some gooey Wonka creation, and she sees for the first time, bloody, prunelike, screaming at this world as if she already fully understands the breadth of its injustice, her perfect thing, her creation, her Josie.

She decides once she recovers and once the baby is ready to be exposed to normal germs, she is leaving. She tells Ellis in bed one night and he thinks she is kidding, then realizes she is serious and says, "I can't leave now. I just, I mean I can't." He's at a crucial point in his novel and he needs to fucking focus. It's going to take several more months, and then there's revisions, letters to agents... "Come on," he says. "Please see where I'm coming from with this."

She stays another week. One day she comes back upstairs from dish duty and the baby is gone. Ellis is out back smoking. She stomps downstairs and grabs a big knife from the kitchen and stomps up two flights of stairs, past her own room, to Swain's, where he and two of his harem girls are admiring Josie. On her stomping, flapping ascent she feels the kind of anger where you consciously decide to channel all the anger you've ever had, in the name of doing something you have to do, every time you've been pissed and incapable of taking sufficient action, anger not just that your baby's been taken without your permission by the kind of people who would have you sit through long supercilious meetings about every vague sociological nothing, nodding their heads like birds, but also anger at your husband's childish pretentious dreams, anger at yourself for allowing yourself to be put in this situation where you've had practically no control over anything that's happened to you the past nine months because you liked the way it felt better without a condom, because he could go longer without the thing scrunching all up and him having to jerk himself off on your thigh; anger over all the shit with your mom from years ago, how she'd bawl into your shirt that it was the stress that killed your father, the stress of living with us; anger over times people were snotty with you at the shoe store. Anger about Reagan. Anger at people who'd yell "nigger" at your friends from cars. Anger at the guy who followed you halfway home at 1:00 a.m. that night going, "Girl I just wanna have a conversation with you, why you gotta be like that…" Active anger felt so much better than passive anger. Like getting enough food and exercise vs. starving yourself to stay thin.

Swain is sitting in a yellow rocking chair, in brown slacks and black shoes with gray socks like a real minister, holding Josie and looking at her like she's some kind of amusing animal. Two skinny girls with long straight hair, one brunette, one dirty

blonde, watch with adoration Swain's adoration of
the infant. The blonde—Shelly or something?—has
both hands behind her arching back and her chin
up, B-cups peeking just barely out of the neckline of
a homemade dress, and the brunette, Jeannie, with
her tan arms poking out in both directions, is sitting
on her hands. Josie at this age always has this look
of neutral wonder when she isn't screaming, her
eyes darting goofily back and forth like fried eggs
sliding around in her pudgy mass of a face.
Caroline puts the blade up to Dennis Swain's cheek.
His face is round, itself fairly babyish, and his hair
is a politician's lame brown lump, firmly combed
and staying perfectly in place, seemingly without
any product. When he looks up at Caroline, his blue
eyes convey to her true surprise and vulnerability.
He delicately passes Josie over to her. Caroline
breathes heavily, her chin up, eyes bulging. As the
baby gets closer to Caroline, the knife gets closer to
Swain, until Caroline has a solid hold on her child's
warm football of a body with one arm and is
pressing pretty hard into Swain's pretty face with
the knife in the other hand. His flesh is pale and
gritty, like sand. Nearly unconscious with fear and
anger at this point, Caroline flicks her wrist up,
nicking Swain just a little. A fleck of blood splats
across his right eye. He puts his head down and
looks up at her with dead eyes and frowns
theatrically, then stands up. Caroline quickly backs

out of the room, waving the knife at the three of them. All this shit she's seen in movies somehow working.

She hurries down the stairs and out the door, all while frantically cooing at Josie. Outside, the gate is locked with a lock she's never seen before, and there is razor wire atop the fence. How many days has she stayed inside? She manages to get Josie under the fence via a small depression in the ground, probably dug by a wild dog, and she starts, with her sneakers and little white chicken bone arms to scale the fence. People drive by, not seeming to notice. A semester of ballet freshman year allows her to get her left leg up over one loop of the wire, but then she is left in a sort of closed-scissor-shaped position at the top of the fence, one leg in, one leg out, whole body wobbling, Josie wailing below, and Caroline thinking, *Aw, shit. I have set my baby down on the ground and gotten myself stuck in an impossible position however many feet up away from her, whatamIdoing*—she thinks this even before she notices the one gray-brown mangy dog speeding towards Josie like a cannon, its ribs visible all the way up from the fucking sky.

She twists her other leg all the way around and gets it into a notch on the front side of the fence, what little fat she has on her stomach pushing super hard up against her ribs. She grits her teeth.

Her eyes get wet. She can see the dog sniffing Josie now. She breathes and a muscle spasm shakes her leg, just before she can do a good jump, and she is knocked off the fence. A piece of razor wire rips through her jacket across the side of her torso. She lands on her back next to her daughter, scaring the dog away. She gasps for several minutes as if coming up from some warm black undertow, her vision fading to gray. Her t-shirt black with blood. Dirt and grass and a woman yelling across the street to a child. The sky, a blue and pink gradient, product of an idiot savant God with an excellent understanding of His color wheel and maybe not too much else.

Caroline picks up Josie and limps to the bus stop and takes the bus straight to Ellis's parents' house and tells them everything that happened and basically begs them to let her and her baby live there and also to consider forcing Ellis to leave that weird cultish house. Mrs. Grand says of course, let us see the baby and go straight to the bathroom, down the stairs and to the right and just make sure we don't have to take you to the hospital for that cut, but that Ellis, you know, it's hard to make him do anything he doesn't want to do. Which Caroline knows is not really true, but what was Caroline going to do, argue? Criticize Mrs. Grand's parenting?

Ellis leaves the artists' colony and comes back to his family after Swain tries to go down on him one night after a meeting. Caroline goes to law school and starts working as a legal aid, making enough for the two of them to move out of his parents' house, and for Ellis to stay at home with Josie. He finishes his manuscript during Josie's naps, goes through years of rejection letters, and then his depression gets worse. Refuses Zoloft on vague philosophical grounds. There are days when he doesn't get out of bed all day and Josie, even as early as age six, pitches unbelievable fits which Caroline is left to deal with on her own. Josie breaks things, locks herself in her room and says, "I wanna die! I'm gonna commit *su-i-cide!*" and Caroline feels the same anger she felt at Swain all those years ago, and even smacks Josie across the face a few nights, after hours-long post-dinner brawls about absolutely nothing, Josie knowing so perfectly how to get Caroline worked up, both standing their ground for impossibly long out of sheer pride, until something long-lasting and emotionally damaging like that happens. And all the while, Ellis is in the bedroom thinking, *I am a worthless piece of shit for not getting out of bed, but I am incapable of getting out of bed due to my status as a piece of shit.* When Caroline comes to bed at night, he says nothing. Some nights she sleeps on the couch.

As a teenager Josie is aloof and her relationship with her mother is strained, only blowing up occasionally, but always cold. Caroline takes her to Paris one week and Josie seems to enjoy the Louvre and the snails and cannot contain her excitement towards the Catacombes, but huffs and rolls her eyes the rest of the time and complains about how much homework she's going to have to make up, which, come on. In college she only responds monosyllabically on the phone and is boy-crazy, which, Caroline thinks, fine, good for her, get it outta your system. Josie takes seven years to finish her undergraduate degree, changing her major a million times until she finally winds up with Cultural Studies, which, what even is that?

Now she works at a pet store. A pet store. For all that, a pet store.

But there are also wholly flawless days of Caroline's life as a mother, days where the air is that special kind of breezy warm, and Ellis gets up and mows the lawn, and Caroline makes beans and rice, and Ellis and Josie build a pillow fort and they all pretend to be saber-toothed tigers in a cave together, and Caroline and Ellis take turns reading *If I Ran the Circus* and *Are You My Mother?* and *The Runaway Bunny* to Josie.

Caroline runs for city council and wins a seat. She has an emotionless affair with a clerk in her office while Josie is away at college and, wine-drunk, tells Ellis one night at dinner through choked sobs, and he responds by finally seeking out the freedom he had wanted all those years ago. She doesn't stop him.

Chapter 9: Human Fly

Josie, in a little pink dress flinging her skinny unexercised body around; Phil, the only one there for the first time in maybe a year. And he's sitting on her bed now, so. But. It's been one whole year of guys with classic loverboy names like Johnny and Armando and Dashiell and Hunter. And also almost definitely his friend Jimmy. She is dancing to "Human Fly" by The Cramps. Her eyes and lips beckoning/ plaintive/ maybe a little mocking. Mocking herself, the world, definitely Phil, and he can't get enough of it. The floor is bare wood and the song is percussive and mean and repetitive and pounding and Josie took ballet, Phil is pretty sure, when she was like nine. Phil is beaming like a goddam idiot. He has had one glass from a $12 bottle of Shiraz. She bends and jumps and tips. He wants to just go over and pick her up, but he would never interrupt the show.

She stops and sits on the bed.

"I'm sweaty and disgusting."

She is glistening and radiant.

He says, "*Noooo.*"

Imagine having to hear yourself say such a thing!

She chuckles and gets up and gets some tortilla chips. She stuffs her face with them and says, mouth full, "You still make that one face when you do it?"

Everything is pink.

Chapter 10: How to Nail an Interview at a Hot New Start-Up Without Vomiting

"Here at Zazz.com, what we're ultimately aiming for is the total annihilation of culture," the man says. His pale brow, little rectangular glasses, and grin give him the look of a confident murderer. "Art, music. Like a physical disintegration."

Phil's attention is divided between the man's speech and the surrounding office, the latter of which is like a child's nightmare of malicious avarice: a gumball machine occupies one corner, and there is a pinball machine in another; dozens of action figures hang from the ceiling on tiny strings—Hulk and The Punisher and Nick Fury and Wolverine, hovering, grimacing, always seeming to stare at you in their stupid, baldly menacing tough-guy way.

Also taking up some of Phil's attention are thoughts of Josie, who broke up with him in February 2012, after two years together, and with whom he has hooked up four times in the past month. He is thinking about asking her to marry him. He thinks he is making progress. Four times in one month, after all, is not bad. It is nothing to sneeze at. She told him she was proud that he pulled himself out of the depression he had been in just after they'd broken up; she said she was proud of him for being so mature and responsible. Of course, the only thing that had cured that depression was the fact that they were spending time together again.

He feels he needs to be a grownup for her now, to start being able to plan a life with her. She has dated men ten, fifteen years older than her, before and after their relationship. She always complains about what a "manchild" her father is. This job Phil is interviewing for is maybe not his ideal job, but what is? What if Phil being consistently employed is what ends up assuaging the anxiety and fear of commitment and general emotional wildness Josie's been going through the past year or so? What if he can make the wildness—the bar fights, the weird dudes calling her at three in the morning, the fuckups at work—stop by getting a job and being the kind of mature person she deserves?

Both men are seated in beanbag chairs; the interviewer's is considerably larger than Phil's. Beanbag chairs allow you to neither sit nor lie down, only to wriggle and squirm in a sort of stomach-aching limbo. Phil must have crossed his legs fifteen times by now. He's in a gray flannel suit. The interviewer wears cargo shorts (brown and frayed) and flip-flops. He has one knee bent and his other leg is resting atop it, so one of his feet is poking out towards Phil, a basically bare gray-yellow foot pointing in Phil's face like a one-eyed monster in a 3-D movie.

"Via new media strategies and rock-star-level personal brand innovation, our site allows users to appropriate content to an unheard-of degree. A sample in a rap song, this t-shirt I'm wearing that shows Mario and Yoshi doing it...it can all be appropriated to become an expression of your personal brand. That's all our generation is capable of. Our company just takes it to the logical extreme. Ultimately there will be nothing left. Which is true anyway."

"Yoshi," Phil repeats.

A beautiful woman with a longish face and nose, which is slender and sloping in a stunning way, walks in in pretty much a doll's dress, short and orange and outwardly poofing and frilly. She is also wearing white stockings up to her knees and the kind of shoes pilgrims wear and a pink bow in her shoulder-length black hair with bangs. Another bow is wrapped around her tiny waist. Her teeth are like the "After" photos in those ads for invisible braces. She kneels down (when she kneels, white underwear peeks out from under her dress), kisses the interviewer on the mouth, hands the two men each a watermelon-flavored Krazybooze™ alcoholic energy drink, giggles, and leaves. The interviewer smiles at Phil in a way that flattens and squishes his red, sparsely hairy dewlap of an extra chin down further.

"We're a, heh-heh, different kind of company than you might be used to," the man says. "There's a water slide downstairs, free candy on Thursdays, and we *don't* serve vegetables in the cafeteria. Last week Andrew WK performed for us."

Phil must be doing a bad job hiding how unimpressed and kind of horrified he is, because the man continues pitching the job's benefits, even switching to a more antagonistic, negative approach: "Listen, you wanna be a, uh, substitute teacher the rest of your life?" he asks, looking on his phone at either Phil's resume or anything else. No, Phil does not! Last week he was pelted with a barrage of colored pencils and accused of racism for using the phrase "colored pencils."

The interviewer is making too good of eye contact now, and sweating a lot. The power he projects is especially interesting considering how incapable, or unwilling, he seems of concealing the more base aspects of his physicality. His voice goes soft. "It's time to play with the big boys, dude. It's okay to want things. Maybe you think it's wrong."

Phil thinks he might become ill—from anxiety, from the stomach pain of trying to sit up attentively in a beanbag chair, from the taste of Krazybooze™, from this man's weird questions and assertions which, although general, feel like personal intrusions because they happen to relate so precisely to Phil's current situation, not to mention the man's equally intrusive, Hobbit-like foot bobbing up and down in front of Phil's face. Phil can't imagine spending another minute here, let alone enough time to get trained, work, save money, get health insurance, propose, get married, meet everybody here, go to company picnics and softball games and holiday parties and happy hours, find a new job while still working and also continuing the business of being a married grownup with possibly kids and possibly a house with a lawn and groceries, give notice, get letters of recommendation from people, possibly including this guy, finally quit...

But Josie snorts when she laughs. When they used to get upset at each other, she'd be like, "Well, let's go get some ice cream," and they would. She likes to walk on the concrete dividers in parking lots, holding both arms out for balance. She has a slightly crooked front tooth that's just adorable.

Phil shakes the man's hand. He hears himself saying, "I can't wait to start." Things are going to change.

Chapter 11: Caroline, No

The office in the past year—2005—has assumed a sort of bird's eye view for Caroline since her election to city council. The office is a little cardboard-and-felt maze of appropriate jokes, black-and-white-comic strips, memorabilia, ephemera, pictures of people's kids' faces and dogs, increasingly printed on company paper rather than developed, pins and ribbons and racks with the little plastic nubs on the end, red and yellow and blue and green, promotional mugs full of endlessly dissatisfying coffee, powdered cream, paper cups, holiday shit, cookies left around, little rubber Martians and bunny rabbits atop pencils, shiny black leather shoes, affordable skirts with extravagant floral patterns, signs busybodies have typed up and printed on company money: PLEASE WASH DISHES WHEN UR DONE WITH THEM THANX!!!!!! ☺

David Hedger, Office Rake by all accounts, comes by around noon every day and moons over her, makes this face with big sad eyes and lips you can almost see tremble like he is *in love with her*, and she talks at him about *The Bachelor* or something else she wants to talk about but knows he's not actually interested in. He nods his head and gives a dead-eyed smile and goes, "Uh huh!" Apparently he slept with Nicole from Demographics, and Caroline has heard he's strongly implied the same, how *dare* you, about Kristina from Accounts Payable as well. He is twelve years Caroline's junior. Apparently he lost like forty pounds before he started here, and is good-looking for the first time in his life. *Awfully* good-looking. Technically not her subordinate. Hairy. Has dropped things like, "A woman as attractive as yourself."

She *knows* she's attractive. She sees herself in the mirror every day and she looks like a ruddier Meryl goddam Streep for Chrissakes and no one else even *tells* her. Certainly not Ellis, who at this point is so depressed he actually *shit the bed* once because he couldn't bear to get up. Other women, when they forget their lunch and have to come back home in the middle of the day, catch their husbands making a different kind of mess. How great would that be? She'd be happy for him, honestly. Caroline has lost her husband in the greatest sense, the sense that she still has to see him every day and lie next to him every night, a shuffling, self-righteous zombie. He got her pregnant when he was handsome and wore cowboy boots and spouted dreams, and every time during

Josie's childhood where Caroline started thinking seriously about leaving, Ellis would turn around and cook spaghetti or put on a puppet show with Josie or get Nick Cave tickets and a babysitter or at least want to fuck all night, which he was capable of until sometime around the beginning of the Bush administration. Things were better when the President was all about fucking.

Mostly Caroline plows through the sexual frustration, and the absence of Josie, who's away at college and who has been emotionally absent from her for years already, and the absolute moral outrage against Ellis's defeatism (which she knows, she *knows* is partly because of a disease, but she can't help it). She plows through these things by working late and getting up and going to the gym and not missing a single city council meeting and getting groceries and picking up jackets from the dry cleaners and seeing every single movie and, last year, volunteering for the Kerry campaign, answering phones, in one of those big bustling dusty rooms full of guffawing zinging men and boys in sensible shirts, two nights a week. It's surprising how little you think about such powerful rage and wanting when you're that busy. It's even more surprising how much you think about not thinking about it.

Caroline has also found herself fascinated by the Internet, how its potential for diversion and information is matched only by its content's subjectivity and shadiness, its danger. It's her kind of library, she thinks, the library the world deserves, one in which everything can be wrong or prurient and there's sometimes no way to know when that's the case. Thanks to Google, she's discovered more than she ever thought she would hear again about the cult she escaped from just after giving birth to Josie: Dennis Swain went to jail for tax evasion and resisting arrest two years after Caroline left. When they went through the compound, it was in shambles: a bunch of the girls were really drugged-out at this point, a lotta crack, and an infant was buried in the backyard. No one owned up to having birthed the baby but Caroline bets it was that bitch Jeannie.

After he got out of jail, Swain ended up working as one of those creeps who try to sell you magazine subscriptions door-to-door. He's planning to launch a career as a motivational speaker. There's this whole documentary you can watch about it on RealHistory.org now. Before, Caroline would passively notice, but not seek out, news related to Swain's compound, or colony (compound is what the documentary called it) but now that discovering as much as possible about it was within her control on a little device at home *and* at work, she could make herself even more busy with this ghoulish hobby whenever she had a free moment. She couldn't hear enough about it, couldn't stop thinking about fresh-faced, Hitler-haired Swain, his lithe girls, his garden, his bellowing rants, the invigorating feeling of doom and menace.

She finds herself alone with Hedger one happy hour, everyone else *said* they were coming. Everyone's always conspiring to make you have sex. It's still light out, and it rained earlier, so you can see outside the street's concrete is just a bright yellow reflection of the sun, dimming everything else inside and out, making the bar, which is Irish-themed, all bright gray. Hedger has two whiskey gingers and Caroline drinks a Diet Coke. Hedger starts laying it on with the eyes and the vague compliments and Caroline needles him about carrying on with Nicole and about hopping into the sack with Kristina. He puts one of his fingers near her mouth. She says, "You are sexually harassing me."

He goes, "Go home with me."

His tie, still on tight. Those baggy pants they make men wear. His big right hand attached to a complicated watch. She hasn't had anything to drink but the overpowering sexual longing from having his finger touch her face makes her swim.

"I'm not gonna *do* that," she says.

"I get it. I mean, but you want to, right?" he mumbles assertively though his substantial eyebrows, making direct eye contact.

"Mm-huh." Nodding her head vigorously, avoiding eye contact for the first time in the conversation. And blushing, reader.

"You're bored, dissatisfied."

"No, see, that's not it. I just believe really strongly that you keep your life together, and—and you don't fuck it up. When I went to college, my mother stopped speaking to me. I worked in a shoe store for a long time where they made me clean out the toilets and rich women tried to get me in trouble. I got pregnant when I was too young and too poor. I escaped a cult—you know about that, right?"

"Yeah."

"I went to law school. I raised a kid. A super-pretty, super-smart kid. I'm happy to be alive every goddam day. I'm happy my baby girl is alive. I'm even happy my dumb fucking garbage husband is alive. I'm an American. I'm an office manager and a city councilwoman. It's the twenty-first century. I'm an American. To want any more would be monstrous. To want any less would be pitiful."

She laughs self-consciously and sucks up the last drops of her Coke and feels like she did good. She adjusts her dress.

"But you do want more. You want me. And that's okay. You deserve *something*. I mean, all those things you just listed off that you're thankful for—you tried to get them and you got them. You can have anything you want. I'm offering myself for you to do whatever you want with. So why not?"

"Why would you do that?"

"Because that's what *I* want. I wanted to lose weight, because I wanted people to admire me for it. I wanted to stop thinking girls were making fun of me, like they used to in elementary school. I wanted to take Nicole out for sushi and make out with her in a parking garage and whatever else, because she's so pink and because of the way her hair is dyed. And also another time, Kristina was around."

"Ugh."

"And I want you, because you have these amazing eyelashes and this powerful mass of hair, and you strut around the office confidently..."

"Ohh!"

"I mean it! And you can have me whenever you want. You can be devotedly faithful to this man and his health troubles or whatever, this man we never see, forgive me, or you can divorce him and, like, go hang out in Vegas or something—but think about it. Isn't what I'm offering more... pro*portional* to the amount of work and trouble and effort you've gone through in your life? Shouldn't you have me?"

She laughs. They're playing with each other's hands now.

She says, "In my heart I know that's bullshit. But thank you."

She gets up. He does, too. Roxy Music is playing. He takes her hand and waist as if to dance.

"You never *stopped* being in a cult," he whispers into her ear. Or maybe it's "stop."

She puts her head against his chest and they dance for a moment. She breaks free and stands there, burning for several seconds, head down.

Reader, she doesn't let him take her home. In a few weeks she will, in the middle of a workday, go up behind him at his desk and insist he take her. They will go to his unnervingly sparse apartment downtown. His roommate will be playing a hockey video game in the other room the whole time. But tonight she has to do something proud and reckless and pointless. She has to refuse, walk out, and feel good about herself for ten seconds before she gets to her car and puts her fist through the passenger-side window.

Chapter 12: Jimmy Resplendent

Every morning, Diya Patel lays her flannel pink PJs out on her bed before she goes to work. She runs and showers and eats a grapefruit with Splenda and packs her lunch, a Trader Joe's microwaveable rice and broccoli affair, and pours some black tea in a thermos. She's an elementary school teacher, so you can imagine how unspeakably early this all is. Today the kids are working on telling time and counting money. At this age, much of the day consists of things like playtime, free play, free choice, recess, second recess, snack, lunch... She seems to remember the Hobbits in those books having a similar schedule. All of her sisters called her a dork for liking those books in college—she was a sorority girl, not like where you all live together and get hazed, she'll make a point to quickly explain, more like just an organization where you sell cupcakes and cookies and raise money to continue the existence of that organization, and they refer to each other as sisters and wear the same double-entendre-laden t-shirts on those cookie-selling days and it goes on your resume or whatever. Shut up.

The teacher's lounge is crazy small and wood-paneled and covered in fliers for yoga classes and dog walkers. The feeling is like a bunker, which Diya kind of likes thinking of it that way. You have to maneuver around the other break-taking teachers' hips and flowy cotton skirts and pants and elbows and around anything that protrudes from the counter—the big knob of the arm of the sheet trimmer, for instance, can knock the wind out of you if you don't notice and run into it, or you can send a mug flying the short distance across the room. Once Diya and her coworkers spent a break, a la *Jaws*, comparing bruises, cuts, even a burn from an errant mug of hot coffee, all accrued from knocking into things in that tiny room.

Diya sees and makes brief small talk with Allison Jennings, who teaches fourth grade. Allison is a few years older than Diya. Her parents are Scientologists. She is the only other unmarried woman on the staff, and she flirts shamelessly with waiters and waitresses alike whenever the faculty goes out for margaritas. They talk about the employee email being down.

She goes home and puts on those PJs and feeds Jimmy Carter, her tuxedo cat, and snuggles up with him and watches *The Voice*. Her roommates aren't home and she laughs loudly to herself and to the cat when Cee-Lo says anything crazy. Nicholas David sings an excellent version of "Free Fallin'."

She watches the local news until the commercial break, then says, "Okay, baby," to Jimmy Carter and takes him to bed with her.

She falls asleep and dreams of her mother yelling at her, just saying the most awful stuff, she doesn't remember what, but relentless. They're in the house she grew up in, which had wall-to-wall fuzzy brown carpets and dark green walls and a lot of Venetian blinds, but they're the ages they are now, and Mom—her thick eyebrows, her round body, her traditional dress—is just letting loose, the way she's only done a few times in Diya's life, the time she got her tattoo in college and the time in high school the cops had to take her home from a party that got busted in the Bluffberg Hills. Vicious, cruel, bombastic, unfair. "I don't do anything bad like that anymore, Mom! Why are you yelling at me? I didn't *do* anything!" Sobbing, consciously infantilizing herself. But Mom won't let go, and they only serve to make each other angrier, for what feels like hours. Diya, in the dream, slams doors, breaks dishes. She wakes up panicking, the palm of her hand imploding like a dying star so she just has this grasping desperate claw now. She manages to clasp the glass of water by her bedside table and take a kava root pill and chase it and go back to sleep. You might think these kinds of things are supposed to hit you in some revelatory moment of extraordinary challenge, but that's not always the case. They get you when you're most vulnerable.

·

Jimmy is at an interview for a job at Bluffberg Public Schools. He likes kids and the pay is good and Phil helped him get all the paperwork done. Jimmy has been working increasingly fewer shifts at Chicken Time, where the nightmarishly pockmarked manager once bellowed at him in the cooler for twenty minutes for calling a female customer "ma'am." Jimmy has mostly been surviving off of Trevor's snacks. Now he's in this long yellow room and five people are looking at him and reading questions off laminated paper. He's wearing a suit and tie and the tie keeps managing to twist itself backwards and he has to keep fixing it.

When Jimmy was six years old, his mother was confident he had Asperger syndrome. She kind of diagnoses everyone with autism. It's a hobby for her. Sometimes Jimmy averts his eyes from people that he's not trying to sleep with, and sometimes he lacks empathy and just talks about whatever he wants, even relentlessly, in social situations. But Jimmy will tell you to take, for an example of his incredible sensitivity, the fellow at this interview with the male-pattern baldness, gray hair, tropical-themed tie, and Philip Roth eyebrows, who asks him about majoring in English. Jimmy knows asking about somebody's major in college is a pretty typical interview question, but to Jimmy the man is really saying: What were you *do*ing? Weren't you listening to the *world?* Didn't you *think* this was going to happen to you? Every boss at every retail job you've ever had, every red-faced friend of your uncle's, guffawing as they strongly implied, between swigs of Heineken, how worthless you would soon be? People *laughed* at you. They laughed in your *face.* Didn't that mean anything to you? How could you possible be so arrogant as to major in English? You knew you weren't going to be, like, a professor, right? Did you think you were going to be Kurt Vonnegut? Were you *so sure* you were going to *blow everyone's minds* with your little thoughts and meanderings? Did you think that because you once rhymed 'cocaine' with 'hydroplane' in a drunk rap battle with Josie Grand that you were going to become some luminary? Look at you, in your orange blazer and your sneakers, twisting your tie around. Hang yourself with it, you dilettante."

Or the super-friendly older woman in a big maroon sweater who asked what Jimmy would say his greatest weakness was. To Jimmy, she's saying, "Tell me about your complete inability to have a simple friendly conversation with a person. Tell me about your issues with your mother that probably freak everyone you know out so much, like what *adult man* has *mother* issues? None that anyone ever wants to be around, is the answer. Tell me about your bordering-on-problematic drinking. Tell me about that rap album you're totally going to make really soon. Have you written a word of it? What do you rap about? Bitches? Money? Being harassed by the police? I can't *wait* to hear it. Tell me about your wife leaving you at the age of twenty-four. Tell me about your eating habits. Tell me about fucking your friend's ex-girlfriend. Tell me about not even being able to."

Or you could take, for yet another example of Jimmy's debilitating sensitivity, the Latino man with the little blue glasses who either said, "Why do you want this job?" or "Listen, you smug bastard. I'm here and you're there. I got here first and I'm going to lord it over losers like you every day for the rest of my life. I'm rude to cashiers, I'm tall in front of you at concerts, and I will make sure you stay in the trenches of pseudo-homelessness and self-hatred and artistic frustration, covered in chicken bones, until your untimely death."

Jimmy surprises himself, though, and answers each question or perceived question as follows, respectively:

"As an English major, I spent four years immersing myself in classic and contemporary literature and its analysis. I was a T.A. my final semester. I'm fascinated by communication in general, and this fascination has led me to an interest in education. I grew up with a little brother who's always needed a lot of guidance. I feel that in college I learned how to *learn*, and how learning works, in a way that I hadn't before. I'd certainly consider pursuing another degree, one in Education, in the foreseeable future, but I wouldn't trade my B.A. in English for anything. I mean, I got to read the *Inferno*. What more can you ask for?" Jimmy smiles warmly in the direction of the lady in the sweater and she gives him a matronly scrunched-nose smile like, "That's adorable."

"Workaholic. My name is Jimmy, and I'm a workaholic. Ha!" At which one of the interviewers, the one with the ruddy face and close-together eyes and comb-over, actually smiles and tips the mug he's holding at Jimmy, as if the mug was full of work.

"The same reasons anyone wants to get into education—it's altruistic at heart, but at the same time there is also a sense of fulfillment I'd compare to artistic fulfillment. Being a T.A. and helping my troubled brother, I have gotten a feeling I think is only comparable to the feeling I used to get writing verse in high school and college. The feeling of imparting knowledge to another person in an effective way is hugely, hugely rewarding."

Jimmy shakes everyone's hand. He thinks: I didn't get it. There's no way I got it.

•

But he does get it! He gets a letter in the mail telling him to contact HR, and HR has him drive out to the blue-gray edge of the suburbs, carefully following the GPS Daniel let him borrow. He is there at 9:00 a.m., gets fingerprinted, peeps the other weirdos lining up for part-time public school employment, their sweaters, their ties with guitars on them, their earnest faces: another world. Jimmy's first day they put him in a classroom full of bustling, energetic little penguin-shaped humans with fresh haircuts and screaming mouths who assault him with hugs for *no reason at all*, and a chubby, Indian-American teacher, with vast reserves of darkness in her eyes and a feather tattoo poking out of her shirt sleeve, sings a song about the weather.

•

It's winter in Bluffberg, so the cold is inescapable, palpable, and still, after living your whole life here, at times, unbelievable. It's as humid as it is in the summer, so it feels like you're swimming in cold water. After spending a minute outside, you invariably have the thought, "Why does it still feel like I'm swimming in cold water? How *can* it?" You think, absurdly, that it will stop at some point, blow over, like closing the fridge. It's like if you could be baked with cold. All the babes hibernate and all the good-looking dudes pair off with them arbitrarily, leaving us uggos to fend for ourselves in the cold, for the duration of the winter. Dads make the same jokes about how they though there was supposed to be global warming. Same winters, same dads, same jokes. No snow, no sleet, no hail, little ice. Winter here is mercifully brief; it's followed by a several-month period which is less cold but too gray to be called spring. It is typically not winter that is a true test of a relationship but summer—in winter, it's just too goddam hard to get out of the house, let alone find new people to have sex with. You need another human for insulation. Your apartment won't protect you. You can't move. You need someone to watch Netflix with, night after night, and drink whiskey. You need to switch off walking four blocks to get coffee and oatmeal. You need someone to walk with you the six blocks to the Triangle and get coffee and terrible burgers and good fries and wonder what everyone else has been doing for the past six weeks. If you can still stand each other when it gets warm out again, and suddenly you're sweating on each other, inhabiting space close to one another that could potentially be occupied by a rare breeze, if that still works for you, get married.

Today, NASA plans on launching an unmanned space thing. It's mentioned in passing on the news, but footage of it is streaming on the NASA website, and Miss Diya puts it on the projector. The launch is delayed, and the two presenters on the NASA video feed—interns or something, Jimmy guesses, because they're really young and awkward—become obviously physically uncomfortable because this wasn't supposed to happen and they don't know what to say. Diya turns the TV off, gets the class's attention—bum-ba-da-dum-dum!—and teaches some subtraction. Jimmy and Diya talk at lunch about it briefly—"You remember the Challenger exploding?" she asks. "How old were you? Me too! Thank God that shuttle today was unmanned, but I was still a little worried showing it, like some reflex, you know what I mean?"

That night Jimmy has to stay after with her and meet some parents. "Just this once," she says with apologetic praying hands and bared teeth, and he says, It's all good, I have nowhere to go.

If you were to make a graph of Jimmy thinking about fucking Diya, the x axis would begin with their first meeting, in the classroom, with the fairly innocuous thought, "She is attractive and I would like to fuck her, if that were ever a possibility, which it most likely, I realize, is not." Were Jimmy's thoughts ever recorded, this same thought would have been cataloged as having re-emerged just slightly after every single interaction he had with Diya: after she flashed her amazingly white teeth in a near-winking smile towards him, after asking him for a favor or commenting on a student's behavior.

The thought, "It is possible that I could fuck Diya, although I don't know how I would necessarily begin to pursue her in an active way, plus I don't really intend to, because I like this job and these past few weeks it's felt good to act something like a mature person, I respect myself a little bit more and I don't want to ruin that, even if I am kind of bored, and also the increase in self-esteem I get from having a job is sort of a variation on the increase in self-esteem I get from having sex with a person, so what does it matter anyway," came when she put her head on his shoulder for like two seconds during an anti-drug assembly.

Coming out of that meeting in the incredible cold, Diya sees she left the lights on in her station wagon that morning, and now her battery is dead. Calling AAA and waiting for a jump is not even an option; she has six layers on and the cold penetrates all of them. The wind is hard and fast and relentless. You can't talk, you can't think. She asks Jimmy to drive her home and that's when he first thinks, "I intend to sleep with the teacher I am assisting." When she comes out of her room in pink flannel PJs and starts kissing him after a glass and a half of $3 chardonnay, he feels something other than excitement at sexual opportunity, other than safety from the coming cold, something reflected in the fact he not only stays over every night for the next month, but also carpools with her, gets big into ordering Chinese and pizza and Indian and watching *The Voice* with her, doing his best Cee-Lo impression at the top of his lungs to her absolute giggling, shushing delight, introducing her to his better-behaved friends, cuddling her cat Jimmy Carter, making him dance with his front paws, talking seriously about IEPs and which kids have fucked-up parents but also about their own childhoods, their own terrible mothers, cats they've had. This is the warmest he's felt in a long time. As they both start falling asleep, Diya wonders aloud what happened with that shuttle launch, but neither she nor Jimmy ever end up looking it up.

Chapter 13: Does Jimmy Sincere's "Pizza on my Blazer" Signify A New Era in Hip-Hop?

By Matthew Elmer, TuneCave staff
4/20/2013, 8:03 a.m.

"Pizza on My Blazer," the first mixtape from Bluffberg-area rapper Jimmy Sincere, begins with a sample from, of all things, "A Prairie Home Companion," the fogeyish NPR folk and, ahem, "humor" show. The sample is host Garrison Keillor announcing, as he apparently does every week, "Well, it's been a quiet week in my hometown…" This clip, in true Beastie Boys fashion, lets us know the stodgy radio host's quiet week is over and Sincere has come to rage in our house for the next half hour. One can imagine Keillor coming back to his quiet, small-town prairie home after a long day of droning into a can and seeing, to his absolute horror, Sincere and his boys trashing his, Keillor's, place, spilling 40's, leaving pizza around like it ain't no thing, scratching all his Mahlers. Sincere immediately confirms my interpretation of the use of this sample with a TOTALLY UNIRONIC record scratch sound, as the title track explodes into the Zune that takes up so much unnecessary space in the pocket of my Levi's 501 Shrink-to-Fits, which I wear about three days of the week, and which I am partial to when I am writing.

I'm listening to the mixtape while sitting in Awful Larry's Coffee Shop in Brooklyn, which has an excellent selection of scones, but the service of which leaves...

[PORTIONS OMITTED]

...Indeed, Sincere's voice ranges from a nasal whine, to a sort of atonal quack, to what can only be described as O.D.B.-esque attempts at throaty, melodic singing. The joy Sincere gets from rapping (and, perhaps, from creating in general) is evident in his carefree style: he will machine-gun internal and external rhymes for a whole verse straight, then fall back, letting the next verse be a series of arrhythmic jokes and ejaculations. English major-y puns abound: "Bitches call me science fiction/ They want that Philip K. Dick." On "Mom," Sincere rails about his family and his upbringing over a piano loop: "Y'all got no idea how Dickensian my life is!"

The day I speak to Sincere, who I've known since middle school, is also the day of the Boston Marathon bombings. The same day, YouTube wins a lawsuit against Viacom, two Earth-like planets are discovered 1200 light years from Earth, and my roommates Landon and Bradon are taking bong hits in the other room while watching *Tree of Life*, a film I found overwrought, ponderous, and, perhaps most offensive of all, totally lacking in the kind of...

[SEVERAL PAGES OMITTED]

"I don't know," Sincere shrugs, his perennially slumped shoulders draped in a big white t-shirt. "I just, I was living with my mom, then living with my friends and working at this chicken restaurant? Like pretty much homeless. And I felt like I had to stop fucking around and really make something honest. I got super pumped one day, I dunno, I got inspired."

"What changed?" I ask.

He pauses, pursing his lips in thought. "I dunno. I've been seeing this girl. She's an elementary school teacher. God, I sound like a fucking asshole. Cut that out. No, whatever, keep it, I don't care."

Chapter 14: Why Are You Here?

Jimmy's duties at school include distributing juice packets at snack time, monitoring during lunch and recess, and reading to the kids every other Reading Time. Every morning he has to go to the front desk, take one of the pens with the fake flowers taped to them out of a little red apple-shaped mug and sign in. It takes a full week of consecutive work days for the secretary, frizzy-haired, freckled Ms. Spiro, to say, "Hi, Jimmy," and not "Can—can I *help* you?" just like that as if Jimmy was some kind of alcoholic dad, or, like, a pedophile who was really, really bad at planning. "Hi, I'm a complete stranger, I was hoping to have some alone time with some of the kids?" Spiro is out every few weeks and the same woman fills in for her every time, someone who wears adult braces and polo shirts and fake eyelashes. He still has to explain himself to her every time.

Diya's closest friends work at the school and are named Jenny Tamblin, April Swardson, Sarah Rhodes, Jenny Allison, Allie Friedberger, and Allison Jennings. They are perfect skin and perfect teeth and long skirts and nondescript long hair and

cross   necklaces   and   little   heart   pendants.
Anniversary gifts from ruddy, chubby men in polos
and slacks. Raucous laughter and weirded-out
silence at all the wrong times. What Josie would call
basic bitches. Allison Jennings is the exception—she
is slightly more tan, she is single, her skirts show
more leg and she drinks more when they all go out
and she laughs at Jimmy's jokes and touches his leg
and leans towards him when she does. They all
know about Jimmy and Diya, and Diya assures him
they are not scandalized by it. They and the
husbands go out to H.W. Sportz's every Thursday
and Jimmy secretly hopes no one he knows sees
him there. Jenny Tamblin says, "What do you want
to do, I mean, ultimately?" He has trouble
answering. "What was your major?" Suddenly
people his age care about this stuff. "So you didn't—
you don't have like a teaching accreditation? So…
why are you here? I mean, why are you working
with us." Jenny Tamblin says this and he also has
basically the same conversation with Jenny Allison.
These women are doing the thing those "How to
Pick Up Women" tapes tell you to do, putting him
down in subtle ways to his face, except the ultimate
goal here does not seem to be seduction, just
making him feel shitty, to put him in his place.
These are women Jimmy's age. Did they not grow
up in the Clinton administration somehow, when
everyone was going to be an artist when they grew

up? It's not part of what he and Diya teach, but he remembers distinctly someone, in school or something, saying to him repeatedly, "YOU CAN BE WHATEVER YOU WANT. YOU CAN DO WHATEVER YOU WANT." Really? I can be like Coolio and Jay-Z and the Notorious B.I.G.? Because those are the guys that I like.

Meanwhile, "Pizza on my Blazer" is getting increasingly more attention. This dude, Prentice Johnston, whose label, Obtuse Records, put out Li'l Baby's first mixtape, contacts Jimmy. Prentice had heard about Jimmy from Matthew's TuneCave review, listened to "Pizza on my Blazer," and would "love to have that sick-ass energy in [his] studio." Prentice's uncle owns a mansion with an ornate recording studio—Prentice sent pictures of microphones that look like something from *Star Trek*, a huge soundproof room, keyboards and slick acoustic guitars with the round plastic bodies, those Dave Matthews-type guitars, big drum sets with yellow wood blocks and purple cowbells and those metal dealies that go *swoosh* when you run your drumstick through them. The place is like two hours east of Montego Bay, in Jamaica. Jimmy is looking at this email and then he's looking up at Diya getting ready to go to work, her shirt sliding up across her torso and then in a big bunch over her head, slightly rustling her shiny brown hair. She smiles at him. Those eyes again, eyes for him. He can do this—he can take the time off, go record the album and come back, sext Diya from Jamaica for a few months. He doesn't have the money, though, and Obtuse is obviously running a pretty low-rent operation. He would have to buy his own plane ticket, the email says. Speaking of rent, he is still paying rent on his new place and he would have to find a subletter or something. No, he can't do it. It's okay, though. He closes his laptop. Diya says, "What?" He pulls her in close and smooches her and goes and puts pants on. Still dark out.

Three days go by and Jimmy hasn't accepted or declined the email's offer. He and Diya make gourmet mac and cheese for dinner. They watch *Girls*. They fuck, still with a condom, but with lots of foreplay, mostly mouth stuff, which Diya is super-great at because she refused to fuck her high school boyfriend for three years. They argue about the end of *The Corrections*, and then fuck again. She rubs his belly as he falls asleep. They go to the farmer's market. They drink coffee. They sing along to "Bohemian Rhapsody" in the car. It's spring now.

Jimmy and Diya get to work on Monday and, as always, Diya goes straight to the classroom and Jimmy has to sign in. Spiro's sub is there again. Jimmy really thought this time she would recognize him. It's been like five times. Again she says, "Can I *help* you?"

When he and Diya fuck, half the time Jimmy remembers this mischievous face Josie once made when she pulled her underwear down with her skirt still on. The other half of the time he imagines fucking Allison Jennings, her tiny ass. He imagines coming up behind her in the breakroom and her just going *wild*, sweating, heaving, up against the table, moaning, no one moans in real life. When he falls asleep he thinks of that email. He thinks of going to the Caribbean and making a real album and being somewhere people want him to be.

He takes a long, dead look at the substitute secretary, who has asked him—AGAIN!—if she can *help* him. Her eye starts twitching. He says, "No," and turns around and walks away, out the door, to the bus stop. He can hardly breathe.

He doesn't tell Diya where he went. She will panic and yell frantically at the secretary until the secretary admits someone with messy facial hair did come in and stare her down and leave. Diya will sit and cry in a chair in the office for ten minutes. She knew it.

Jimmy goes to his apartment, replies to the email, buys a ticket to Jamaica for tomorrow (he has a credit card now) and packs haphazardly. Never tells his new roommates anything, either.

Because *come on*, he thinks. She recognized me. She just wanted me to know I wasn't welcome there.

I had been working there for months. Fucking *months*.

Chapter 15: Dance on the Bones 'til the Girls Say When

Josie is sitting on a bench waiting for Henry, who she considers to be an archetypical bad boy, in the classic Shangri-Las vein. If she ever had to write an essay again—she misses it—she would write about how we need the archetype of the bad boy in pop culture to live vicariously though, to dignify the tough and independent struggles of the working class—or perhaps, conversely, to caricaturize them, to make them ridiculous, to turn them into totally unbelievable, clearly fictional cartoon characters—and to endear us to the kind of male sexual rage that pervades the world and might otherwise make society in general inclined to exterminate teenage boys en masse. We're attracted to media types, she thinks: recall girls in college swooning over the *most* tattooed dude, the hipster with the biggest glasses, even the really specific ones, like the guys in black suits who were big into old soul records, or Beat poet wannabes. They were just so devoted.

Henry is authentically bad because he has mentioned owning guns, and she's seen him get into three fights—one at a house show, one at a wine tasting, one at a sci-fi convention. So often bad-boys turn out to just be slobs or rich kids or mentally ill people but she is sure this is not the case with Henry. He told her his father beat him and threw him out of the house when he was fifteen. He worked his way through college to major in psychology, but dropped out halfway through because he decided he cared more about—get this, for real—the job he was working at the time, which was working on cars. Strong, bony face. Tattoo sleeves—a lightning bolt and an iguana and a big blue swirl and a line from Bukowski in typewriter font and a naked babe in a glass of whiskey. He has the biggest hands you've ever seen.

Henry said it would be really funny if they got super coked-up for the thing tonight. The thing tonight is Apartheid people getting together for another bonfire in the woods. Josie is not a big coke person really because she has sensitive sinuses, but she agrees it is a funny idea. The bag is in her jacket, which is this old yellow leather jacket of her mom's she found in the attic recently. She has her hair in a bun and a little skirt and bike shorts. She absently purses her lips and stares at her legs, which she hates because they are pale and stumpy. Other things she hates: her upper arms, her slouch, a slightly crooked front tooth. She realizes she didn't eat anything today: she had been late to work and forgot to bring a lunch and decided to just get coffee on her lunch break.

Henry pulls up in the Cutlass and says nothing. She likes the way his silence compels her to come up with things to say. Jimmy was a whirlwind of unpredictable speech patterns. Dashiell and Hunter both talked a lot but were boring as fuck and habitually shouted down her cultural analyses with their more boring ones. Phil still stares at her and asks her questions about her life the whole time every time they hang out, which is exhausting.

"What'd ya do today?" she asks Henry. "'Zat a new shirt? You get my texts earlier? What's your favorite animal? Do you believe in God? What was middle school like for you?" They snort the coke off the dashboard at a red light.

At some point Josie makes a joke about how awkward and clumsy it is when he takes off his cowboy boots in order to have sex—to clarify, these are *cool boots*, but when Josie's tiny frame is up on him and she's squirming around and smooching all over his mouth and face and neck and maybe he's running his huge enormous hands all over her torso, at some point the boots have to come off unless this is like a tabletop or kitchen sink situation, which never happens as often as she'd like due to wariness of roommates or just general convenience, as in they're already in the bedroom, and so the whole boot process pretty much 100 percent kills the romance/ naughtiness buzz because of the amount of time and awkward, clumsy physical exertion it takes, which is actually *fine*, and *cute*, but also worth mentioning in joke form, Josie thinks. In retrospect, joking like this is uncomfortably close to the way her mother would criticize something she doesn't like about someone to his or her face in order to avoid confronting the person in a serious way, but the joke ends up being poorly-timed and unfunny and therefore just fucking awful for everyone involved. Henry just says, "They're good boots," furrowing his brow and making his lips puff out a little.

"Are you up*set*?" Josie asks, laughing. "Are you actually *mad* at me?"

"They're the only boots I have. I mean, what do you *want* from me?"

"Um, I want you to stop *yelling* at me, for one."

"I wasn't yelling at you."

Henry drives up past the shopping center with the clock tower in the center, past the skate park that's being torn down, past the new '50s-style diner. He takes the exit to 238, over the Waffle House, sun still setting, and out past the mansions and their vast expanses of perfect green lawns. Both in the car are silent, hearts pounding loudly, unpleasantly. Josie's left eye is twitching and her arms are crossed and she sighs repeatedly.

"It's this one," Josie points to the dirt road coming up on her right. Henry grunts and makes the turn. A strong fire burns in the distance.

Kaylee and Marie and Jay from Apartheid all think Josie moving from their store to a pet store that paid better and on time and where she had more responsibilities was lame, although Kaylee, who has fuzzy black hair and favors high-top sneakers, is more insistent on it. Marie, the store's buyer, sends out the mass texts to these bonfires, and always hesitates to invite Josie, in part because of the scene Josie's friend made that one time, but also in part because she no longer really keeps in touch with them otherwise, and she didn't even work there for that long. Just as they're talking about all this, a big gray old car comes crunching up through the woods, its obtrusive blue light flashing unflatteringly on all their faces. Josie gets out of the car and makes "L" shapes with her arms to present to the crowd the gentleman who drove her. She shrugs and says, "This is Henry, y'all." After a brief pause, Kaylee jumps up and squeals and hugs Josie and says, "Guuurl!" Josie reciprocates with only slightly less enthusiasm.

Henry stays quiet this whole time, except when the two are whispering forcefully to each other. Josie sucks down like five cans of Miller High Life and Henry nurses one. After a lot of work talk among the current Apartheid bunch, politics come up and Kaylee says, "Well ah just think this whole Obamacare thing is just ridiculous. You wanna get taken care of, you get a *job*." Marie says, "I don't really agree with you so let's just try and move away from this subject…" but Kaylee pushes it until both stop talking, and then you can only hear bugs and the fire's crackle and Henry whispering to Josie: "Because you see me as some kind of novelty. The kind of life I live, for you it's some kind of vacation from the terrible thoughts you have all day about yourself and your future and your parents, and from the energy you have that's not being put to good use. You listen to *self-help tapes*, for Christ's sake. I grew up in a certain way and choose to live my life in a certain way and it's a diversion for you and you think you can just tease me relentlessly like a fucking—like some trained animal, and it's fucking bullshit."

After a while Jay gets up and stretches, his veiny arms protruding from a sweater with a kitty cat on it, and says, "Alright, guys," and says his goodbyes: "I'll see y'all tomorrow. Josie, see ya. Sir, it was good meeting you." In this blurry moment it doesn't matter, but in a little bit Josie's head will be clearer and it will occur to her that Jay is totally leaving early instead of coming out and telling her and Henry that they are making things super uncomfortable for everyone. Kaylee and Marie hug everyone and each other and get out of there soon, too. Josie is crying a little by that point and fury is just emanating off Henry. Kaylee and Marie, opening their car doors, give each other the same face where they grit their teeth and bat their eyes, then get into their cars and drive off. Josie says, "Don't touch me. I'm leaving. I'm just gonna go, I'm just gonna walk home, it's not that far."

"Not that far? What?"

He touches her arm and she wriggles wildly until she's on the ground, then gets up and stomps away.

"Josie. JOSIE."

Henry starts walking after, the fire behind him is the only source of light, save the moon. Trees smack against his legs and arms and face. Josie is walking faster and faster, her skirt swishing around, and Henry can see her legs getting visibly more scratched-up. This is so stupid. He is cold and crashing, half-asleep. He can't do this kind of thing for much longer, especially not for some girl who he's only been seeing for a couple weeks and who has just been humiliating him for the past several hours. Life can't always be like this. He is not afraid of trouble, he tells himself, but he can't fucking stand having his time wasted. He could be home, drinking the whiskey on the floor next to his bed. He could play with his roommate's new dog, hold a stick over his head and let the brown muscular pup jump up on him and stretch out with its paws on his chest. He could call Carli and see if she wants to hang out, if she's off at the titty bar. He could play his bass. Any of those things would have been a real good night. He trips on a log and now his jeans are wet. He calls out for Josie again and hears a distant, "*Fuuuuuck yooooou*" in reply, and he turns around and walks in the opposite direction.

Josie is surrounded now wholly by sublime darkness and pain; the night wind is exhilaratingly cold, and thorns and twigs and noseeums and mosquitos and branches whip and peck and bite and sting and attack her at unexpected intervals, no predicting it, like Chinese water torture, maddening…She marches on and on, stomping, her feet wet, shoes smacking against cold mud and dirt, grimy socks sopping up against her endlessly cold feet, surely black and brown by now. She feels blood run down her legs, an outside, invasive force feeling her down even though it came from inside—obtrusive, presumptuous. Who said you could crawl down my leg like that. Who said you or you or you could smack at me and hit me in the face and legs, who said all this fucking dust could get up in my nose and these tears could tickle my cheeks, I will destroy you all. I'll get a bulldozer as soon as I get home and I will come for you. Her fat stumpy hateful legs are failing her but her lungs are *great*. She could breathe in and out forever, she could breathe in dust motes all day long, as well as moths, salamanders, dogs, gorillas, buildings, Republicans, her parents, your insecurities, this novel, the patriarchy, words, atomic bombs, diseases, gold, America, all of history, all of humanity's suffering, in and out, altering none of it but letting it course through and empower her as she stomps.

The moonlight shows a break in the path with a deep ravine, gray in the night, several feet down, seemingly endless in both directions. She scales down it, front out, arms back, shoes digging into clay. She walks through almost-freezing water, Jesus fucking shit it is cold for this time of year, whatever. She splashes, she could stop and wipe her legs and arms off, but she doesn't care, it is time to go home, there is no time, she is racing against her stupid legs' inadequacy and her increasingly crashing head, her sleepy eyes, fuck that, she is coming home. She falls in the water and hits her ass, a monstrous, full-bodied sudden shock of pain, unprecedented, like the first time you ever got hurt, and now her whole skirt and part of her shirt are a freezing, twisted, gnarly fucking mess. God dammit. She swings her left arm up out of the water and throws her body up against the night. She penetrates the soft clay of the other side of the bank's wall with her hand and pushes herself up, swinging one leg over the side, flopping her stomach on the dirty ground. She feels like trash. She feels like she deserves to be down there. She is losing power, her lungs not so good anymore. It feels like when she would run the mile in high school. She can't get up now. She is wet and covered in wet stuff and caked in filth and losing all this blood from her legs and so drunk and crashing so hard and so hungry and so so so so so so tired. She wants to crawl but even her arms are revolting against her. She closes her eyes, black juxtaposed with black, endless expanse of night vs. endless internal, eternal expanse: no difference. She is caving. All the fighting has been for nothing, her whole life, her mom's whole life, because here she is, on the floor of the woods, totally powerless, like a baby.

Oh well. She has had her adventure and now she is alone, like we all end up anyway, alone. It's so cold. Before she drifts off to sleep there in the black woods, she thinks she can see the dawn.

Chapter 16: Olivia Benson

Emma Marie Sincere lies supine on the couch, resting up and flipping channels post-dinner, trying to find *Law & Order*. She likes Detective Benson, likes how she's strong and beautiful, darkly beautiful like a lake at night when the moon is full. Likes how she doesn't take shit from anybody. All this frantic, manic flipping and searching, through basketball, through *To Catch a Predator*, through Honey Boo Boo, through the house builders, the fisherman, C-SPAN of local political hearings, channels she doesn't get, Pay-Per-View sex stuff, the radio stations, '40s, '50s, '60s, '70s, metal trash, R&B trash, rap trash, hippie trash, all of it reminding her actively that life is a dark narrow path through an awful wood, where you're alone but surrounded on all sides by fear and disability and disappointment. You're surrounded by illness and death and random catastrophe and men who are wanton and frightening and powerful. You're surrounded by poverty, by bureaucrats, by government bureaucrats who try to get between you and your check, by the uselessness and depression of your two sons, one you haven't heard from in almost a year, the other in his room down the hall, lights on, blasting that grating techno music, almost certainly lying down, just like she is, only probably touching himself or working on his stories or both at the same time, but either way dreaming, always dreaming. Probably also thinking about that bitch girl he was so obsessed with, the one who worked with him at the yogurt place, who, when Emma had come in and asked to see Elvis, the girl laughed and asked if Emma was serious. Skinny. Blonde. Nothin' special. Elvis could do better if he would just pull himself out of that hole he's been in, she knows it. He has big white tubular arms that could almost be mistaken for muscular if he didn't wear those baggy clothes; he's kind, he's sweet, he's funny, he's smart, he's *imaginative*, he likes to have fun, likes to laugh…Has her nose, unfortunately, but that's okay for a man. The other son, she was just trying to be helpful, just trying to put things into perspective, we can't all be a rapper, and we certainly can't do it just by hanging out with our fancy college buddies and leeching off *her*. That's what she said to him and he threw a drink in her face and left. Two boys. Two boys who used to go off in the woods and play together, even though Elvis was afraid, Jimmy would show him how to ford the stream, where to find salamanders—that was just after Stan died. The only man who ever said he loved her, the only man who ever said, "I wanna give you sons," and Jimmy and Elvis were too young when he died to understand beyond "Mommy's sad" or "Daddy's not here…" In addition to her usual physical torpor, she is now almost paralyzed by emotional pain and sorrow from reminiscing, and Detective Benson is nowhere in sight. The fat gray cat, Biggy, starts crawling all over her. She says, "Oh, look who's the sweet one *now*," and extends her hands to pet the cat. Biggy swats at Emma's hand, draws blood, and Emma calmly picks the cat up and drops it to the floor. She goes and knocks on Elvis's door and sure enough, he is lying on his back on his bed, hands behind his head, wearing a plaid button-up shirt and cargo shorts, and his t-shirt has one of those cartoon ponies from that show he likes so much. She lies down next to him on the bed and picks up his right arm and moves it so it's around her shoulders. "Tell me what Olivia Benson is up to," she says. "Tell me a story about her."

Chapter 17: Carrie

Phil walks out of Zales jewelers and he has a parking ticket. Like, what the fuck is the meaning of this. Like, fucking, how *dare* you even. Sure, he had parked his new used 2005 Prius a *little* over the yellow line in front of the store. Barely. Like he doesn't have enough to worry about, he thinks. Like he didn't just buy this car, for instance, or buy this *diamond ring* for a girl who is definitely seeing other dudes, badder dudes, dudes with tattoo sleeves, he understands. That's what she was doing last night, he's pretty sure—hanging out with that dude, at one of those campfire parties he always used to get so sullen about going to because he felt excluded from the work-talk, felt insignificant. Now, he thinks, he probably wouldn't even care, because he believes in himself. He's gotten *many* supportive emails thanking him for his contributions at Zazz, from inside *and* outside of his department. He's been a part of several teams, he's networked, he's created content, *so* much content, he's spearheaded things. You name it. Turns out that's all it takes to make Phil like himself. That, and occasionally sleeping with this girl he wants to spend the rest of his life with. All that's great. But this ticket? This is fucking infuriating. It's like, really, life? This after all he's done? After all the money he's already spent? After the great but also awful year he's had? Great in terms of what he's done for him*self*, awful in terms of what everyone else has tried to do to him? Parking tickets, shitty friends who take advantage of Josie's temporary craziness and temporary availability by boning her (well, one shitty friend, or rather, one friend who might be autistic and whose tendency to just do whatever he wants Phil kind of admires...), boring parents, the humiliation of job interviews, a stressful hookup experience plus a series of fruitless attempts at online dating, including several instances of women standing him up, women he didn't even want to meet in the first place, whom he didn't even find especially attractive or charming in their pictures and profiles and brief instant message conversations... Plus, struggling against his own personality. Most importantly, his triumph over himself, over the lame-lord Josie dumped.

It's okay, he thinks. He's on his way to do something that will, he's sure, make him happy for the rest of his life. He knows he can calm down. He can pay this ticket. Of course, it's all more than worth it. He gets in the car.

Phil notices he's almost out of gas, which—God, he really needs to just cool it. This gain in confidence has created an impatience in him, a desire to fly off the handle at every inconvenience. It's just gas, and he'll go get it, that's all. "You expect so much," his mother might tell him in a rare nag. "You expect to just jump into the professional world, you expect to just park however you like, you expect for there to always be gas in the car and for the world to acquiesce to your idea of absolute convenience, like some king, you expect to go over to the apartment of the girl of your dreams every week or so and have her fuck herself dry on top of your boring dick…"

In his head, he thrills to respond to the dream-mother, the mirror image of a woman who would never really use such language or criticize him so thoroughly, he responds: "Hell fucking yeah I do."

He always has been, and always will be, Mommy's Special Baby. She drove him to school every day when they lived a block from the school. Prepared him oatmeal every morning. Fought his battles for him, against Todd Jenkins, who threatened to beat him up at the bus stop, and against Miss Kerner, who said he wasn't allowed to write a book report on *Ender's Game* in seventh grade because it wasn't serious literature—Mom went and found several critical studies of the book. That kind of history about himself used to fill him with self-loathing, but now that he's doing well, he appreciates it, sees how it gives him a competitive edge over other people, over co-workers, over dudes Josie hangs out with...

Phil goes and gets gas, and the attendant has trouble understanding him say, "Forty for the Prius over there," even though what else would he be saying, come on, man. He fills the car up and closes the lid and throws away the receipt and buckles in and starts the engine. He backs out of the station in reverse and hears a disgusting thud behind him. Phil has backed into somebody.

The man has greasy hair, tattoo sleeves—Phil thinks he can make out, in the brief moment he's looking at him, a lightning bolt and some typewriter font words—and a tight black t-shirt and blue jeans. The man is on the ground, and his white disposable coffee cup has spilled all over next to him. His hands are huge, Phil notices. Looks like a real "bad-boy." The man's back is to Phil so he couldn't have seen him or his license plate. The man starts to get up and Phil drives away, turns a corner, hears curses yelled at him from the street, but he's gone.

•

Josie is lying in a pool of blood. Or rather, a tub full of water, into which has seeped, like red streamers, some of her blood, from out of the cuts all over her legs and from stomping through the woods last night and smacking past thorns and branches and finally passing out on the ground. She looks just like Carrie, covered in blood, the beautiful blue wide-eyed gaze Spacek gave to every scene, a lost baby animal, so shocked that the depths of the cruelty she was experiencing could exist. "But I *wanna* go, mawma!" Perfectly thin (recall Carrie was fat in the book), that chiseled angular nose, the frightened face turned only slight to show psychic rage in the prom scene. Better in that movie than any silent film actress, better than Clara Bow, better than Musidora, better than Garbo...

This morning Josie had found a clearing that led to the highway, walked along the edge of it (any time you see somebody walking along the side of the highway, or by an exit, that has to be the low point of their life, right?), caught a bus, and walked ten blocks to her apartment. Impossibly, shatteringly thirsty the whole time. Hair a nest. Sucked water out of the bathroom faucet for several minutes once she got into her beige bathroom with the weird drawing of Jesus they got from Transfiguration Thrift hanging over the toilet. Her dumb black skirt she might as well throw away at this point—it was only thirteen dollars—but her mother's old yellow leather jacket is still strong. The cuts sting when she first gets into the lukewarm water, but to rest even for a moment, to soak, is intoxicating, and she begins to think about Henry, how he left her there in the woods, what a perfect fucking dick she must have made of herself, haranguing him, mocking him, defending herself pitifully against his accusations that he is just a prop for reinventing herself as a bad girl, which he is, when all he wanted to do was go out with her and her coworkers to drink some beers, poor guy, poor smart strong handsome guy who all he does is work, work away on cars, wearing a little shirt, getting dirty, wrenching things, wiping sweat off his brow, probably taking off his shirt, that huge expanse of chest, unlike anything she's ever seen, those tattoos swirling around his arms in psychedelic testament to nonchalance towards pain and permanence. How in the gray night he picks her up and moves her. How he works her tirelessly, expends her in his massive saurian way, without thinking, just grunting, his flop of Clark Kent greasy brown hair flailing above his dead eyes. The pink water splashes underneath her, she stretches her arms and legs out, pawing at herself as an extension of the initial relaxation, her body's pulse amplified by the water the same way water amplifies sound...

Someone knocks on the door. God dammit. Come on I am almost finished with this. Just— could be him, though... Could be him and he could finish her off. Josie doesn't watch porn a lot, although she did an extensive research paper on it in Advanced Critical Studies 501, and this is just masturbation thinking anyway, but it could be Henry, or it could be anyone, the way male porn actors pose stiltedly as mailmen, pizzamen, the classic repairmen, any of these freakish goateed muscle monsters becoming bashful when confronted with her shamelessness as she opens the door... Of course these thoughts only make her go at it harder, ignoring the knocking. A final shudder and she closes her eyes. Very briefly, she feels a sensation of absolute self-loathing, followed by an extreme, general malaise. *Fuuuck.* I better answer the door. God, I'm awful. God, I'm gross. Covered in viscera here.

It's Phil at the door, fumbling with a little black box. Josie is like: I know what this is. He doesn't seem to notice or care that she is in a towel or that she has cuts all over her legs or that she is covered in a thin layer of what must be impossible to mistake for anything other than blood. All this time, working at this awful job, he must have been saving for this. Geez. Her best friend, who takes care of her when she gets too drunk, who listens to her talk about other boys, who always wants to go for ice cream, such a good, good, good, good, good, good boy, when she can see now that what she is a husk, a horror movie monster with bad legs. She hears herself saying, "Yes. Yes!"

Chapter 18: "An Investment in My Future"

Ellis spends most of his time walking around the house absently. He looks at the birds in the yard, he puts his hands in his pockets, he sings along to "Rock 'n' Roll Animal." His depression has subsided lately, except for the occasional attack at night. He hasn't worked for months, but he is on disability and social security and unemployment, and Caroline still has to pay him divorce money. His daughter is getting married tomorrow. He goes on the Internet a lot. He reads about lizard people and Jewish conspiracies and gold and 9/11 and JFK and aliens. Sometimes he clicks on the ads: "If you don't speak Spanish, watch this video now," with a picture of a Hispanic babe, hair flowing in the breeze, tube top; "VIRGINIA: Obey this 1 weird 'loophole' to lower your taxes now…" with a picture of a sexy accountant looking up at the viewer from under her visor, cleavage hanging out of a half-buttoned white shirt with big lapels, hair in a bun…

Someone knocks on the door. God dammit. Come on I had just—

"Good afternoon, sir, I'm sorry to bother you, I am currently selling magazine subscriptions, a few years ago I got into some trouble but I am fully rehabilitated and trying to make something of myself and get back on my feet, I fully repent my previous actions and behaviors, most people usually buy the subscriptions not because they are excellent magazines at a reasonable price, but as an investment in my future, out of the kindness of their hearts, so won't you please—"

The man gets this far into his spiel before he recognizes Ellis and Ellis recognizes him. Ellis has grown a mustache since the man last saw him, and his hair has grown out. He's grown a huge pot belly, and now seems to favor shorts and running shoes over denim jeans and cowboy boots, but his eyes have the same beautiful brown depth, his nose continues to protrude confidently. Ellis recognizes the man, same brown lump of hair as always, same blue eyes, but his once-babyish face has become gaunt, his skin flaky. He is Dennis Swain, former leader of the cult Ellis and Caroline escaped from, subject of *Tragedy in Bluffberg*, a documentary Netflix keeps recommending to Ellis.

Swain's mouth is slack, his eyes dead. Ellis isn't sure if Swain can tell who he is, or if he remembers him, remembers cornering him in the Meeting Room that night after everybody'd left and exposing himself to Ellis and whispering desperately, *Come on, please, it's okay...* He sure looks like he's been through some shit. But it's gotta be him. Right?

"What'd your say your name was?"

Swain hesitates, furrowing his brow. "My name's Dennis."

"Come on in, Dennis. What's your story?"

Ellis feels swelling inside him, a kind of exhilaration he has maybe never known. Not as a young aspiring poet, not in his current state of freaky, libertarian, Internet-lover's freedom, certainly not as a married father. Ellis loves glamorous coolness and adulation and stoned, relaxed reverie—and he realizes in this moment that he also loves vindication. Vindication against a man who caused his, Ellis's, wife to run under a fence with a baby, a man who pulled out his weird red knob of a dick and showed it to Ellis, who derailed Ellis's plan of a life of bohemian harmony and chores and girls and just working on his poetry, had to derail all that with his rules, his impositions, his presumptuousness, his appetite. All of a sudden fat, depressed, divorced, failed poet Ellis Grand is Clint Eastwood. He doesn't have a plan, but he doesn't care.

Dennis stammers: "I—I lived a hard life. I got hooked on drugs. I did things I regret. I did time in jail. I did things I don't wanna think about or dwell on except to know I have to redeem myself."

Oh, the joy Ellis feels. He sucks up his chest, gives Swain a good long look, and asks Swain why he did those things he mentioned, the things Swain says he doesn't want to think of. Ellis asks if it's maybe because he's a dangerous psychopath who only sees people as, like, receptors of his, Swain's, stupid crazy far-out opinions, and, and ideologies, man. Ellis asks Swain if maybe that's why he did the things he regrets. He asks him if maybe he, Swain, did the things he mentioned regretting, the aforementioned things, because he sees people only as sexual objects and potential audience members and suckers, rather than as whole human beings with souls, who deserve freedom and like, rights. Ellis asks if maybe that's why.

When Ellis wakes up, his head is bleeding and his computer is gone.

Chapter 19: Jamaica

It's dusk, and everything in the Bluffberg Elks Lodge is all brown and green flowers and banners, in honor of Josie and Phil's wedding. Jimmy showed up pretty much on time, as people were getting seated, and gave enthusiastic nods to Trevor and Daniel and Phil. Trevor squinted a second to recognize Jimmy, then grinned and waved spastically. Daniel gave what Jimmy took to be a "Can you believe all this?" smirk, and Phil just smiled a little, clearly nervous as hell. Jimmy smiled at Phil's parents, who both gave embarrassed and confused-looking smiles in reply, teeth gritted. Jimmy recognized Josie's mother from a suggestion by Facebook—strong jaw, bright red lipstick, hair done up in a conical pile, yellow blazer. Beautiful but tough-looking, substantial, handsome. She is sitting next to Josie's dad, that old sheepdog of a dude, and he has a shiner and looks really dazed, like he might pass out at any minute. Josie's mother is twitching and red-faced next to him, like she would happily stab him to death at any minute. Josie comes in in her wedding dress, this little sloping number, not ostentatious like a lot of wedding dresses you see but slim and in harmony with her tiny, bony frame. Her skin is shining and she's smiling this big near-crying smile and her nose is wrinkled up like he's maybe only ever seen her do a few times ever, and he thinks, I don't know these people. I've maybe never known any of these people and I've maybe never known anyone, or myself, or anything. I feel so disconnected from absolutely everything right now. I don't even know how to feel about this, or about anything, for that matter, at this point. This numb ambiguity could either be the prelude to a huge outpouring of emotion, or it could just stay like this forever, or neither of those things, Jimmy has no idea.

The actual ceremony is over pretty quickly. Phil looks like a big dumb penguin or something up there and they both cry and just look really happy, and maybe that's actually nice. Sad, though, right? That this is what it's all been for? All those nights? Really, this? What's the big deal? He can't shake his confusion at all this, and at his own feelings, and that begins to frustrate him.

Jimmy is still purple all over from his trip to Jamaica, and his hair is still braided. Everyone knows he has gone to Jamaica and failed, everyone must surely think he looks ridiculous; everyone must have some idea of how stupidly he must have acted to have undergone this physical transformation. These people. All dressed up and leering and grimacing. It is time for Jimmy's speech; he is best man. He looks out at the crowd, at everyone with their slightly confused smiles— everyone except Mrs. Grand, who still looks furious, and Mr. Grand, who is beaming ecstatically—a look that is contorted, to tragic effect, by the big red bump hanging over his left eye. He looks like some kind of sad troll. Jimmy picks up his glass of champagne and raises it above his head and clears his throat.

•

Jimmy had arrived at Sangster International Airport after arranging to meet Prentice. He recognizes Prentice from his website and also maybe from around town: Prentice's dreads, his long thin torso draped in a Bad Brains t-shirt. Prentice has dead eyes and speaks in a low, conspiratorial tone all the time and has a limp handshake. He uses the words "clean" and "wet" instead of "cool" or "tight" or "sick" like a normal person, and he says "out of pocket" instead of whatever that means. They get in a light blue oval-shaped rental car and Prentice speeds gracefully along the road, darting around big vans, military vehicles, rusted-up old sedans and station wagons, along the long two-lane strip of highway, through thick jungles, then beach on one side, shacks then mansions then shacks again, a huge barbecue pit like a flea market, hundreds of people eating and walking around and waiting in line, dogs running and jumping, goats grazing. The barbecue smells incredible through the A.C., which Prentice keeps pumped the whole time, until the cold is unbearable. Instrumental, organ-y rock buzzes tinnily on the stereo, too quiet, so you can't help but strain to hear it. Prentice tells long, specious-sounding stories about gang violence and haunted plantations and Jimmy gives cursory responses; he is tired and dazed in that way you get when you are far away from everything you know. The road gets increasingly windy and wooded and narrow and steep until they get about halfway up a mountain and Jimmy sees a white mansion. Prentice stops the car in front of a gate where a big guy in a red suit stands, hands behind his back, frowning, neck puffing out under his chin. Prentice asks the guard where he got the suit and the guard, past the window, very quietly, under the tinny music, chuckles and says, "That's very good, sir."

The mansion is like a typical 1990's American rich person's home, sloping brown bannister, lotta white, baby grand, basket of wood fruit, generic abstract art, beige carpets, fireplace, chandelier. Prentice takes Jimmy straight down to the unimpressive basement studio, which has a glass partition and puffy pink soundproofing stuff all over concrete walls. On one side is a couple chairs and a Mac with a huge screen on top of a nice dark brown lacquered wooden table, and on the other side there is that drum set, a big Yamaha keyboard with all these knobs and pedals and buttons attached, a sunburst Paul Reed Smith guitar attached to Marshall stack. Perfect equipment for making like an *Arrested Development* or N.E.R.D. record, Jimmy thinks. He proceeds to spend the next several months there with that equipment, mostly making beats on a series of different computer programs but also using the instruments sometimes, spending hours on the floor hunched over a laptop, freestyling in long bursts, seeing himself get better and better, sampling Roxy Music and Emerson, Lake & Palmer and Fleetwood Mac and Elvis Costello and The Monks and saying, "Can you turn my headphones up?" really just to say it, and saying, "You hear that? You like that? Uh-huh. Wait for it. Wait for it. Uh-huh. Yeah. There it is! And then, wait it goes—okay, here it goes. Oh, shit! Right? *Right?"* Only going to the bedroom upstairs to sleep and sometimes going out back, down the mountain to the beach. Prentice brings Jimmy chicken and beef and noodles and steak and ackee and saltfish and mangos and Doritos and cereal and amazing pot, completely mellow and physical, and coke, and, twice, heroin. They eat together and don't say much. They make faces at each other while eating. Jimmy is full of creative energy nonstop every day from waking until passing out in the big white impersonal bed upstairs, perfectly satisfied, often not even jacking off before sleeping, and when he sleeps he dreams the kind of beautiful absurd dreams you'd have as a kid. Riding on a whale with your brother. Being on a bus, but then you have to get off the bus, but you get to meet Led Zeppelin. You're at a store that only sells hair, and everyone gets a new hairstyle that way, it's just accepted in the world of the dream, and Daniel is there, and your mother, too, and she seems happy. One night Jimmy dreams of walking around in the woods behind his mother's house, the house he grew up in, with Phil, and the dream is so vivid he decides to write him.

"Hey man. I don't know if a lot of people know this but I'm in Jamaica making an LP. Me and Diya broke up. How are you doing? Say what's up to Josie et al."

Phil responds with a two-page email detailing his every responsibility at work. It is like some practical joke. Still, Jimmy is happy to hear from him. He writes back and sends him an mp3 of a thing that isn't quite done yet. Three or four emails later, Phil invites Jimmy to be the *best man of his wedding to Josie*. Which, Jimmy thinks, a) Phil *must* know that Jimmy and Josie got it on a couple of times when they were broken up, because Josie brags about that kind of stuff in front of everybody, so the whole thing seems kind of—what?

Sacrilegious? That Jimmy should, like, officiate this kind of...And plus, b) more importantly, Jimmy has never even referred to himself as a man (except ironically, like, "I'm a partyin' man,") only as a dude or a guy, let alone a *good man*, let alone a man who is the absolute *best of all men*. Why would Phil possibly want this? It must be some kind of peace offering, right? Let's stay friends, it's okay that you fucked Josie, okay that you guys were several times a wild gross ball of flesh feeling around together, without a condom even, because now I am marrying her and you are all holed up in a strange white house on a mountain, in the wilderness essentially. Jimmy goes out to the back of the house, doing that wobbly fall-walk down the steepest parts of the mountain, to look out on the expanse of sand and water, into which the sun seems to explode as it sets, lighting the blue night with spastic yellow and orange. Jimmy thinks about how unfair life is, even though he knows that's not quite the right sentiment for the news he's processing. He starts thinking about God. He hasn't thought about God in a long time. When he was like six, Mom took him and Elvis to church—he barely remembers it—for what could only have been a few months of Sundays, everyone was super old and super nice to him, uncomfortably nice and well-dressed in suspenders and canes. One day he and Elvis started fighting in the pew during a sermon about The Prodigal Son, and he called Elvis a "shitbird" right out loud in front of everybody and Mom dragged them out and yelled at them in the parking lot, didn't stop yelling about how they'd embarrassed her, even after they were both crying—anyways, Jimmy thinks God must be like Pablo Picasso. All He does is make great-looking stuff like this tropical sunset all day, or like Biggie the cat swatting at some gnats in the backyard, or like Josie's stupid cheekbones, but He takes no responsibility for how everyone's life falls apart around Him all the time, even though He could if He wanted to. Jimmy decides that yes, he will be the best man, he will absolutely be the best man, he will be the absolute best goddam man, and he'll show them all.

·

Jimmy is dreaming he is at the zoo with Anjelica Huston. They hear a jackhammer sound and see that all the exhibits are closed due to construction. The jackhammering gets louder and louder and Jimmy wakes up to hear it coming from outside the house, only the individual hammering noises are reverberating in different places all along the front of the house: the house is being shaken by a wave of machine gun fire. The noise stops. Jimmy lays awake the rest of the night without moving.

Early in the morning, he gets up and looks quickly out the window. No one's out there. He goes outside: there are bullets all over the ground but there is very little damage to the front of the house—clearly whoever did this didn't get past the gate. Thomas, the guard, only works from nine to five, so he must be fine.

Jimmy goes to Prentice's room to check on him. Prentice is up and stretching in his boxers. Prentice says, "'Sup, man?"

"You hear that last night?"

"Yeah. Fuckin' scary. I wonder whose house they were after."

Jimmy squints and pauses briefly. "Where's your uncle?"

Prentice walks out of his room, past Jimmy, towards the kitchen. "I told you, he's gone on business most of the year." Prentice gets some OJ out of the fridge.

Jimmy doesn't say anything but leans against the door, looking off in Prentice's direction but at nothing in particular. "Can I hire a choir for one song? I need a choir. Like is there money for it?"

"Sure."

"I need it for that song, 'Paris.'"

"Which one's 'Paris?'"

"The one with the Jerry Lewis sample."

"Jerry Lee Lewis?" Prentice drinks the OJ from its carton.

"Can you just go get a choir for me? Like from a church?"

"Yeah, man."

Jimmy records a song with a choir, along with several hours of sessions with a trumpet player and a sitar player that almost sounds like free jazz except with Jimmy screaming indecipherably, sounding agonized. He takes to wearing a big black robe he found in his bedroom closet over his usual t-shirt and jeans every day. If Prentice was concerned by any of this, there is no record of it. Jimmy has an organ moved and built into the studio and drones away with it over a sound collage he's made of police radio and porn dialogue.

Jimmy's not sleeping anymore. He is afraid of every loud noise, especially his own. One night his worst fears appear to come true when a wooden hollow boom explodes downstairs, boots run upstairs, and his door slams open. Three gray figures stand above Jimmy. "Look I don't know who you guys are but you've got the wrongguyI'mamusicianfromAmerica—"

One figure flips the light on. The men wear cop uniforms with big yellow patches on their sleeves.

"It's gotta be him," says the middle one, who has a shaved bald head and crooked posture. The cops to his left and right take Jimmy's arms, handcuff him, and lead him down the stairs. From the foyer, Jimmy can see six or seven other police walking in and around the house, examining things, looking inside the piano, taking paintings down, rummaging. He does not see any sign of Prentice. One of the officers who burst into Jimmy's room stays behind, and the other two officers lead him to a mostly black and yellow cop car with fins in the back. On the side there is a logo with a wreath with a crown on top of it and the letters "JCF." In the car, the cops argue while a country song plays softly on the car radio.

"But why does Chip go back to his family?"

"Because he realizes his life is like that script, it's a comedy disguised as a tragedy. He feels foolish for what he's done, he's taken himself too seriously."

"I see that in the context of the script he was writing, the way he described it, but what does it have to do with going to eat dinner with the other Lamberts? What does anything have to do with family?"

"I gotta tell you, man, this, you and me, this is the worst book club I've ever been a part of."

"Aw, come on, man."

Jimmy thinks maybe he should seize this opportunity to grab something out of his pocket and pick the lock on his handcuffs with it and jump out the car door, or yell something, anything, to create a distraction that would crash the car, but thinking about it is as far as he gets. He is in a daze, not just from having just woken up, but from having woken up from one of the first good nights of sleep in weeks—weeks?—and having no idea why he's being arrested. Police said something about "racketeering," which, what even is that? Isn't that a good thing? Like the opposite of profiteering? Racketeering sounds like something your mom would take a class in. The road is illuminated only by the two white beams from the car's headlights, nothing else around, just the faint idea of trees, the clueless stars. The gate between him and the cops is rusty, and the seat is that hard sticky brown plasticky-material that chips and gives way to yellow foam. He chips at it as the police continue arguing.

They pull up to a blocky vanilla-colored building with bright blue doors and a fountain out front. The bald police officer opens the door and Jimmy gets up. They escort him past the fountain and into the building, which seems otherwise unoccupied. The first room is harshly lit from above, with white walls and a single desk with papers stacked high, a lamp, three dirty coffee mugs, a big gray box of a computer monitor, and a small statue of a woman in a bikini puffing her lips out and holding both hands behind her back. On the walls are utilitarian, unadorned calendars, some kind of chart with black-and-white computer printouts of peoples' faces on it, and a bookshelf full of binders. The cop with hair—it's got gray patches and is almost at afro length, and he has a mustache, says into his radio, "Taking him in now. No, Sanders didn't finish the book. I know, he's the worst. Next? I'd say '*Freedom*,' but we can do a different author if you want, Lieutenant. Over."

There is water damage all over the cell, huge brown tie-dye splotches like tea that's leaked all over a napkin. There is a cot and a toilet on the floor. Someone has written on the wall near Jimmy's pillow, "BIG MONEY 4 LIFE." Sanders and his partner stand in front of the cell, smirking.

"What do you have to say for yourself?" Sanders asks.

"I don't know why I've been arrested. My name is Jimmy Sincere, I'm visiting from America to make a rap album. You know, hip-hop?"

The officers' smirks disappear. The mustachioed cop steps closer.

"We don't know anything about that, Mr. Burgess. What we do know is that we've had an inside man in your crew for almost a year. We can't say who yet. He gave us your address and this video of you handling cocaine."

The mustachioed officer, whose badge reads ALLEN, holds up a phone with a video of a man partially obscured by darkness and packing bricks of coke into a suitcase. The man is white, with braids like the kind Jimmy got from a skinny hustler on one of his few daytime trips to the beach. The man in the video has a huge nose, much bigger than Jimmy's. Otherwise his face is similar to

Jimmy's except chubbier, and the people who mill about close behind him throughout the video are all much, much, taller than he is. The cops seem to have Jimmy confused with someone who has more exaggerated versions of every physical flaw Jimmy already feels self-conscious of.

"Besides," snickers Allen, "you're wearing a t-shirt *with your crew's name on it.*" Allen and Sanders laugh so hard Allen actually has to lean against Sanders at one point. Sanders dries a tear from his eye.

Jimmy's t-shirt says "BIG MONEY" on it. It has a drawing of two tumbling die on it, outlined with glitter.

Jimmy protests: "I don't know what that is! My friends got this for me when they went to Las Vegas!"

"Las Vegas!" Sanders brays.

"Your friends went to Vegas!" Allen howls. Both cops are doubled over, short of breath, tears rolling down their cheeks.

"Big tough crime lord! Trying to tell me...Oh, God, this is too good. Come on, man!"

Jimmy looks up and blinks hard and gulps, the magnitude of the situation bearing down on him. He tries to run his hand through his hair, but the braids make it difficult. The two cops walk off, still chuckling, and Jimmy doesn't see them, or anyone else, for two days. The light through the window is bright white then gray then black twice, and Jimmy gets hungry, then unbelievably hungry, then numb to the hunger, almost nauseous, then crazy hungry again. He panics about dying in the cell, then succumbs to a kind of hysterical happiness, completely without reason, then indulges again in self-pity. He thinks about bashing his brains out against the wall or with the toilet, or drowning himself, just to avoid starving, in case that ends up being a possibility. He yells and screams. He raps every verse of every song he's ever written, and of every rap he knows by heart, then sings other songs, The Beatles, "The Wheels on the Bus," "I Can Tell That We are Gonna Be Friends," his voice breaking and fading in and out. He thinks over every bad decision he's ever made. He thinks about what he'd say to everybody he knows if he could see them now: mostly he'd tell everybody off for how they've failed him, brought him to this miserable place, how it's all their fault for not being supportive of his dreams. On the third day, Allen walks in and opens Jimmy's cell door.

"Okay, Vegas, you can go. We caught the real Burgess. I'd get a new shirt if I was you."

Jimmy, sitting on his bed, stares and gapes at Allen for maybe thirty seconds. Allen rolls his eyes and gives a nonchalant rapid nod and a "come on out" hand gesture. The thought does not occur to Jimmy to flip out or yell or grab the officer—he just stumbles out, saying nothing to anybody the whole way out of the station. Someone hands him a box with his shoelaces and four Jamaican dollars, and he is outside in the blinding heat and light. He buys a bottle of water and a beef patty from a stand, sucks both down conspicuously, and calls his mother from a pay phone.

•

From the sound of Emma's breathing and the noise in the room, she is smoking with the fan on, which would put her in the den, which has blue carpets and is right now mostly full of boxes of old toys and stuff. Probably doing her crossword. She might be looking at one of the toys that sticks out of the old boxes—a stuffed gorilla with a heart Jimmy got her one Valentine's Day when he was little, an action figure of Spider-Man's enemy The Scorpion, some Legos. "Yeah?" she says. "Jamaica? What are you doin' there? No, you can explain it to me. Explain it as quick as possible. Uh-huh. Uh-huh. Why are you calling? Okay, well I have a few conditions to that." You can just barely hear Elvis's anime blasting from his room, explosions, corny voices loudly expressing dismay, laser blasts, and Elvis guffawing uproariously at all of it. "First of all, you're sorry you threw a drink on my face. Uh-huh. You're sorry about generally behaving like a maniac in my house and you're not gonna do it again. You're going to be a respectful adult. You're going to stay here until you get a real job and you're going to seriously consider taking that sales position Uncle Dave wanted to give you. You're going to at least do the dishes and clean the bathroom. You're not going to act like you're too good for us. You're going to comb your hair. You're sorry. Okay? No, I'm not done. You're *sorry*. You're going to eat dinner with us five nights a week while you're here. You're too old for this stuff. Say it: I'm too old for this stuff. You're not an artist, you're a regular human being. You're not going to be an artist or a rapper or a singer or anything like that. It's ridiculous and ostentatious and foolish. It's not a real goal for a person your age to have. Sales is a real goal. Say it. Say, I'm not an artist.

"Say it. Say you're not an artist. Okay?"

•

An uncomfortably long time seems to have gone by with Jimmy holding his champagne glass up, staring out at the crowd and blinking. Caroline, Ellis, Daniel, Trevor, Josie, Phil, a bunch of people Jimmy doesn't recognize, all look on expectantly. He knows what he should say: that he had sex with Josie four times, once on Daniel and Trevor's couch, another three times in her bed, that he came inside her mouth the first time, that she asked him to pull her hair, that she asked him to slap her in the face, that all there was in those moments was her, how she smelled like candy, how red, her pull, her little

arms weirdly strong, her medium-sized breasts
pointing up at him, the way she would just take her
top off without reservation, how she'd bite, bite too
hard and too often. How she wanted more, wants
more, always always always wants more of
everything, and so should all of you, you pathetic
bunch. Turn that wedding cake over. Smash these
tables. Kill the Elks. We can be so much more. We
are here to celebrate mediocrity today. We are here
to ensure our slow deaths, our insignificance. I want
to be famous. I want to make the Sistine Chapel. I
wanna be Justin Bieber. I wanna be Jim Jones. I
wanna be Charles Manson. And you, people like
you, you are killing me. Seriously, burn it all down.
Or jump up from your chairs and kill me, I don't
care. People will talk about it, people will never
forget it, and then none of us will ever die. Or, I
don't care, move to Seattle. Or get big into
woodworking, or home brewing. Anything, you
monsters, anything.

Jimmy says, "I'm gonna be totally honest. I'm
here because—"

An unearthly guttural wheezing cuts Jimmy off,
and there is a great splash, and Ellis falls off his
chair. Ellis is on the ground vomiting. He stays on
all fours and the sound he makes when he vomits is
like screaming. He is projecting his voice like an
actor, as though he must throw his voice out along
with everything else inside of him in order to get

the bad stuff out. Caroline rushes to his side as soon as he falls, and much of the rest of the crowd immediately gets up and walks hurriedly out of the room. Women grab their purses, even take off their heels in order to walk faster, immediately, as if they'd planned on it. People trip over each other to get out. Another chair falls. There is just an incredible amount of orange and brown vomit, and the smell is mostly citrusy.

"It's okay. It's okay. What's wrong? Why are you vomiting. It's okay, you're okay. Did you eat something other people didn't eat? What is it?" Caroline coos desperately at Ellis, her gloved right hand on his back. Josie stands awkwardly over the two of them, and Jimmy sits back and drinks his champagne and smiles. They are the only people left in the room.

"Mushrooms," Ellis gasps in between heaves.

"WHAT?" Caroline takes her hand off Ellis.

"I took painkillers and then I took these mushrooms I had. Like, you know, the good kind. But listen, I have to tell you about something. I saw him. I saw—"

"You came to your *daughter's wedding high on mushrooms?* Do you realize what you've done? You—*ooooh.*" She smolders for a second, then gets up, pointing at him from above, like he's a bad dog. "Your ego has determined literally every aspect of how my miserable life has gone so far. You just do whatever you want. You—"

"It's not the same. Your disappointment is not the same as mine," Ellis says. He is no longer vomiting at this point, but sitting upright on his knees, his back arched forward, deflated, cummerbund awry, beard all splotchy with orange and brown liquid and chunks. "I wanted to be a great poet. You never wanted anything."

"You think I wanted *this?* You think I wanted to stay in *Bluffberg?* You think I wanted a *surprise* pregnancy? To join a *cult?* To live with your *mom?* To support everybody…"

"Well when you put it like *that…*"

Jimmy is drinking champagne from the bottle and watching as if he was watching a boxing match. Josie turns around and stomps out.

•

She stomps down a recently-buffed brown tiled floor, fuzzy reflection of the rectangular lights above. On the walls to her right are bulletin boards, little announcements, just shapes and colors, cartoon eyeballs, scrawls, numbers. She slams open a big wooden pair of double doors that has bronze handles with some Latin inscribed on them. Inside the room is a standing mirror, a bunch of boxes, some candles, an old TV, and Phil. His bowtie hangs down off his neck. He is sitting on one of the boxes and looks surprised to see Josie burst in, bare arms outstretched, white dress poofing out under her. She walks up and socks him in the jaw.

"Ow!"

"Sorry!"

"You can't hit me! You can't keep hitting people in the face!"

"I know, I'm sorry! You're right! Hey, but *fuck* you for running away!"

"I'm sorry. I'm sorry about that, too. I freaked out."

"You can't run. We can't run from each other anymore, ever."

"I know. I know. That's the whole idea."

"Exactly! We're family now. It's always wrong to abandon your family. Hey, c'mere."

She puts her arm around his head and brings it close to her hip. He nuzzles her groin with his head like a puppy. She spreads her sweaty fingers out across his face and kneads his cheek with them, back and forth. She pushes against his chin and plays with the hair on the back of his neck, prickly-short from a new haircut. By now she is also rubbing herself, in her big frills, up and down against his forehead, more and more fervently. She breathes heavily and her arms feel warm inside. She pushes his head harder and he puts his arm around her expansive white dress and clutches her legs. She pulls the dress up quickly and puts it over him, like a blanket, like a tent, like a ghost costume, and he pulls her underwear down and grabs her ass and brings her pussy in close. He's always been pretty good at this. She lifts her right leg and rests it on his knee, and pushes up against him. She thinks how she will never (really?) sleep with another man but him, will never sleep with a black guy, will never sleep with another big strong guy like Charles Buddy or like Henry, not that she'd even want to spend the requisite amount of time with either of those two dudes to even end up having sex in the first place. Here is a thought Josie has had before: rough sex is basically for white liberals. Although she herself is white and pretty liberal politically, she wants to count herself out of this group she's thinking of, well-to-do kinky people who go shopping at sex stores as if it's fucking Pottery Barn, because they have lots of money and time and they get into this stuff because they don't have a real struggle in their lives, because they don't have to worry about work, like she does, paying bills and rent, like she does. The materialism of it, the consumerism of it, buying different accouterments and guidebooks, it's awful. But she likes what she likes, and so, she thinks, maybe she'd better go get some books. That's all. Grind your foot down against his leg and swat awkwardly at the bulging nub protruding from his tux pants. Flail your hand about trying to find the zipper without looking down. Breathe. Push. Pretend it's wrong.

Chapter 20: Karaoke, in Japanese, Means "Empty Orchestra"

Josie sends out a text to Jimmy, Trevor, and Daniel: "H.W. Sportz's. It's karaoke night. Let's save this thing." Still in her wedding dress, with Phil still in his tux, she drives to the bar, and everyone arrives at roughly the same time. In the parking lot, Trevor runs up and says, "Did you see that?" As though it was no longer important to address the catastrophic wedding they just experienced. "See what?"

"I thought I was looking at like a rat or a mouse scampering into those bushes over there, but I swear to God, it was the weirdest thing, it stopped and looked at me, I could see it really well because the headlights were shining on it, and, a) it was a hamster, like a fat fuzzy orange guy, and, b) its face was bald and really scratched up. It looked like a tiny Yeti."

"No fucking way." Josie thinks: can it be the one she had to flush down the toilet? Robin? Is that possible?

The hamster peeks its tiny, gruesome face (more like one of Batman's enemies than his sidekick now) out of a bush. Josie kneels down and says, "C'mere, buddy!" She takes out a piece of wedding cake she had wrapped up in her bag and offers it a crumb. The hamster runs up and eats the crumb, and Josie takes it in her hand and goes inside with it, clutching it to her chest.

It's clear by now that a storm is coming. The wind is blowing unreasonably, insistently, and leaves and trash are scattering all around and swirling in circles. Josie can feel the first mist of rain on her heels as she enters the bar.

It's all blue inside, and the place is packed with a typical karaoke crowd: some more young people, a pack of old guys, some moms. An Asian girl Phil seems like he's trying to avoid, celebrating her own wedding. That dude, Noah. Oh boy. Jimmy and Josie sit together at the bar, both drinking Stellas. Robin sits at the bar, behind her hand, remarkably calm.

"So, I didn't tell you," Jimmy says. "I guess I'm getting a job at my uncle's store."

"Yeah, no you didn't tell me, we haven't spoken at all since before you left for Jamaica. Remember? You didn't tell anyone you were leaving or anything?"

"Yeah…"

"It's a furniture store, right?"

"Yeah, and actually, I feel pretty good about it. Look at this: 'Hi, ma'am, can I help you find anything?'"

Josie laughs. "Uh-huh. Okay."

"So then you're supposed to say—"

"Oh, okay, I see. Yes, I need an ottoman."

"'Right this way. Ah, these are our cheapest models, and if you wanna upgrade, I can recommend something from our Luxury Collection...'"

Josie laughs. If you listen close over the music and the talking and the clatter of glasses you can actually hear the wind howling outside. Thunder is flashing with increasing frequency, and the rain spattering against the window is intense, violent.

"You know I *like* your music," she says.

"I didn't know that. Thank you, though."

Noah goes up and sings and *kills*. He sings, "I've Been Lovin' You Too Long" by Otis Redding. Josie had no idea he was such an incredible singer, this tall, boring wisp of a guy who used to give her such a sad stare when they hung out. He moans and howls with dramatic anguish, gets down on his knees, all apparently for the entertainment of the girl he's with, tall and tattooed, with black bangs.

"I might start writing for Zazzpop," she tells Jimmy. He responds with what Josie can tell is genuine enthusiasm. "Yeah, Phil and Daniel are both putting in a word for me, and I've got my writing samples all ready: an essay about how my parents were in a cult when I was a baby, an essay about this time recently I got lost in the woods on coke, ha ha, and another about the *Friday the 13th* movies. Hey, who ya textin'?"

"No one!" He snaps his phone shut, but Josie can see he was at least considering texting Diya.

The lights go out, the microphones and the speakers all lose power. It's dark. Everyone keeps singing, for as long as they possibly can.

Acknowledgements

Amanda, Casey Childers, Lizzy Acker, Evan Karp, Mom, Dad, Jai, Theo, Alicia, Sarah Griffin, Ceri Bevan, Lauren Traetto, Katherine Duckworth, Toni Mirosevich, Michelle Carter, Maxine Chernoff, Andrew Blossom, Amira Pierce, Tom Batten, Justin Sink, Evan Hume, Chris Pittman, Jake Ziemba, Paul Krumholz, Amanda Long, Alani Foxall, Carolyn Ho, Kelly McNerney, Justin Kahler, my editor Emanuella Martin, my agent Jod Klemp, my PUA life coach "Heisenberg," and my close personal friends Beyoncé and Joyce Carol Oates.

About the Author

Nate Waggoner has contributed fiction and criticism to *Quiet Lightning*, *Shipwreck*, TheFanzine.com, Write Club SF, *Makeout Creek* and KQEDPop. He has an MFA in Fiction from San Francisco State University. In 2014, *SF Weekly* named him one of the best writers in the Bay Area without a published book. He co-founded The-Tusk.com, a daily website that publishes cultural commentary and memoir. He lives in Brooklyn.

www.ingramcontent.com/pod-product-compliance
Lightning Source LLC
Chambersburg PA
CBHW070933250626
47159CB00009B/3225